"You shouldn't have done that."

"Why not?" he murmured in a husky undertone. "I thought it might bring back a few memories. It certainly brought back a few for me." His lips twisted in an arrogant smile. "You always were a passionate little thing."

A rush of red-hot anger replaced the warm feelings inside her, and she pulled away from him. "And you always were full of yourself," she snapped. "For your information, I hated every moment of that kiss."

"You do surprise me," he drawled lazily, then placed a finger against his lips as she looked ready to explode. "Shh! Don't wake the girls."

Abbie took a step back from him, her gaze moving over the laughing gleam in his eyes. That kiss had been just a joke to him. "I hate you, Greg Prescott...I just hate you."

KATHRYN ROSS was born in Zambia, Africa, where her parents happened to live at that time. Educated in Ireland and England, she now lives in a village near Blackpool, Lancashire. Kathryn is a professional beauty therapist but writing is her first love. As a child she wrote adventure stories and at thirteen was editor of her school magazine. Happily, ten writing years later *Designed With Love* was accepted by Harlequin. A romantic Sagittarian, she loves traveling to exotic locations.

KATHRYN ROSS

Ruthless Contract

Harlequin Books

TORONTO • NEW YORK • LONDON
AMSTERDAM • PARIS • SYDNEY • HAMBURG
STOCKHOLM • ATHENS • TOKYO • MILAN
MADRID • WARSAW • BUDAPEST • AUCKLAND

ISBN 0-373-11807-4

RUTHLESS CONTRACT

First North American Publication 1996.

Copyright © 1995 by Kathryn Ross.

CHAPTER ONE

LIFE never went as you expected it to, Abigail reflected
as she looked down from the plane at the skyscrapers
of New York.

Jenny and Mike had been so happy, had had so much
to live for. For a moment her eyes blurred with tears
and swiftly she searched in her bag for a tissue. She
wasn't going to cry any more, she told herself fiercely.
She had already cried enough tears to last a lifetime.

She could still hardly take in the fact that her beautiful
sister was dead, that she would never see her or Mike
again.

The pilot's voice interrupted her thoughts as he told
them that they would soon be landing at JFK and that
the local time was five-thirty in the afternoon...

A frisson of nerves started to twist inside Abbie as
she thought about seeing Greg Prescott again.

It was five years since she had last seen him. It felt
like a lifetime ago. It had taken her a long time to get
over the havoc that man had wrought in her life. Even
now at the oddest times she found herself thinking about
him, thinking what a fool he had made of her.

The plane touched down smoothly and the long flight
from London to New York was over. Abigail didn't move
immediately; she waited until the majority of passengers
had gathered up their belongings and were filing down
the aisle before she even unfastened her seatbelt.

Then calmly she opened her handbag and took out a
small compact to check her appearance.

Her blue eyes were slightly shadowed, reflecting the fact that she hadn't been sleeping well recently, and her skin was very pale. With a sigh she reapplied dark pink lipstick and then ran a hand through her long blonde hair to fluff it up. She wanted to look completely composed when she saw Greg.

She had been surprised when he had written to her and told her she could stay with him instead of at a hotel, and she had been even more surprised when he had offered to pick her up at the airport.

She had wanted to refuse both offers. The thought of having to spend any time in that man's company was completely abhorrent. It was only the thought of the children that had made her write a stiff letter of acceptance.

Poor little Daisy and Rachel. She bit down sharply on her lip as she thought about the twins. It was quite frankly just the thought of the children that had kept her going over these last few days. She had every intention of taking them home to England with her. They needed her and she was going to be there for them.

Swiftly she rose to her feet, a look of determination on her young face. She was going to have to face Greg Prescott now and forget their past history.

It seemed to take forever to clear immigration. Even though you no longer needed a visa to visit the States, the authorities were hot on who was coming in and, more importantly, when they were going to leave.

Abigail was thankful that she had heeded Charles's advice and booked her return flight in advance. She could always add the children on from this side once she had cleared everything with Greg.

Her heart thumped nervously as she picked up her bag and walked through the barriers. Her eyes ran searchingly along the sea of faces waiting at the other side. At first she couldn't see anyone she recognised and she wondered for a brief second if he just hadn't bothered to come.

She pushed her trolley around the crowds and headed decisively towards the telephones. She wasn't going to stand around like an idiot waiting for him, she told herself angrily. If he couldn't be bothered to be here on time she would make her own arrangements.

It was then that she saw him. He was leaning indolently against a counter to one side of her, just watching her.

Her heart seemed to miss a beat and for a second they could have been the only two people on the planet. The crowds around them, the hustle and the noise just seemed to disappear as she met those dark, deeply disturbing eyes.

He looked different...yet so familiar that her heart leapt crazily. He was still ruggedly handsome, only now the darkness of his hair was flecked with silver at the sides and instead of wearing casual jeans he was dressed in a formal dark suit. He looked every inch the successful lawyer that he was.

He didn't move towards her immediately, but took his time, his eyes lazily sweeping from the tips of her stiletto-heeled shoes over the navy blue suit that clung in a flattering way to the slender curves of her figure, before resting slowly on her face.

Much to her annoyance she felt herself starting to blush and he smiled as he noticed her heightened colour. Only then did he move across to her.

'Hello, Abbie, it's been a long time,' he murmured in that deep drawling tone she remembered so well.

She bit down on the impulse to say, Not long enough. 'Yes, it has... You haven't changed.' It was the only thing she could think of to say to him and it wasn't strictly true. He had changed and it wasn't just the silver strands in his hair.

The Greg she had known was good-natured—approachable. This Greg looked harder somehow—tougher. An aura of power seemed to encompass him.

She supposed the meteoric rise in his career had contributed to the harsh, uncompromising look of his features. After all, Greg had achieved more in the last few years than most men did in a lifetime. You didn't climb to the top without ruthless determination.

His lips twisted drily. 'I'm not sure whether I should take that as a compliment or not.'

'It was just a casual comment,' she shrugged, and looked away from him. She knew very well that he was remembering the rather severe words she had spoken last time they had seen each other. 'Listen, I don't want to put you out in any way.' She continued on in a rush. 'If it would be better for you, I'll just book myself into a hotel somewhere until we sort things out.' Her voice was abrasively brisk; she didn't mean it to sound quite so prickly, but she was very uptight, very uneasy about the whole situation.

He flicked her a glance from eyes that were quite calm. 'Everything is sorted out,' he told her in a low, firm voice. 'I've made the necessary arrangements. The funeral is tomorrow.'

A cold shudder ran through her body at those words.

He picked up her bag and marched forward towards the car-park, leaving her no option but to hurry after him.

'So.' He stopped by a silver-blue Mercedes and put her luggage in the boot. 'Did you have a good journey?'

'It was all right.' In truth she hadn't noticed much about the trip; her mind had been too taken up with thoughts of Jenny, worries about the children and, of course, the dread of seeing him again.

She waited until she was seated in the car and he had started the ignition before she asked the question that was burning inside her. 'How are the children?'

He glanced at her, and for the first time she glimpsed the tired, strained look of grief behind the remote countenance. 'If you want it in one word, devastated.'

Abbie bit down on her lip and turned over-bright eyes away from him. 'I just can't believe it's happened, Greg, I really can't. It's like a bad dream.'

'You're telling me.' Grimly he swung the car out from its space.

They didn't speak at all until he had hit the freeway and they were headed towards the centre of the city.

'How's your mum holding up?' Abbie turned slightly in her seat to look at him.

'She's been very brave. I reckon a lot of it is for the children's sake.'

'Is she looking after them?'

'Yes ... she's moved into my apartment for the time being. She's coping very well, considering, but it's taking a lot out of her.' He raked a distracted hand through the thickness of his hair. 'Luckily I have a good house-keeper who comes in each day, and I intend to try cutting down on my workload so that I can be at home more, but it's difficult.'

'Is that necessary now that I'm here?' she asked quickly.

He gave a dry laugh. 'I can't see you looking after young children.' He flicked a hard glance at her. 'You're hardly the domesticated type.'

Her face burned with anger at that remark. 'I can assure you that when it comes to my sister's children I could become any "type" that is necessary.'

He shrugged. 'But you won't be here long enough to be much help ... will you?'

She let that remark pass in silence.

He turned off at the next junction and was a moment concentrating on the flow of traffic before he spoke again. 'How's that boyfriend of yours—what's his name?'

'Charles.' She muttered the name through clenched teeth, knowing that Greg was going to make some kind of sarcastic remark.

'That's right, Charles.' For a moment Greg's lips twisted in the semblance of a smile. 'I'm surprised you haven't married him yet... You considered him quite a catch, if I remember rightly.' He flicked her a sideways glance. 'What happened? Didn't Mummy approve?'

Abigail glared at him. 'As a matter of fact I get on very well with Charles's mother,' she grated furiously.

His lips twisted scornfully. 'So he just hasn't asked you yet?'

'Yes, he's asked me.' Abigail was so incensed by the question that she answered without thinking. How dared he ask such personal questions? She wouldn't dream of asking about his girlfriend. For a moment a picture of Connie Davis flashed vividly into her mind. What had happened to her? she wondered distractedly. There had been a time when she had expected to hear that Greg had married Connie, but the years had passed and he was still single.

'So you've turned the paragon down?' Greg continued with a wry twist of his lips. 'Amazing... all that lovely money too.'

Abigail was momentarily speechless at such an outrageous remark. 'No, I haven't turned him down,' she grated heatedly, once she had caught her breath. 'Not that it is any of your damn business.'

'So if you haven't turned him down, then you are engaged to him?' He darted a glance at her left hand, unperturbed by her angry tone.

'I'm thinking about it,' she muttered in a low voice. 'If you must know, he asked me a few days ago, just before the . . . accident.'

As she was talking she was wondering why she was telling him this; it was far too personal. She cursed herself for allowing him to get under her skin so easily.

'Why play games? It's inevitable that you will marry the guy,' Greg grated drily.

She shot him an angry look. 'Nothing is inevitable.'

One eyebrow rose mockingly as he pulled into an underground car-park and a reserved space. 'The Abigail I know would never turn down the likes of Charles Marsden.'

Greg really hadn't changed a bit, she thought furiously. He could still bring her to boiling-point with the mere lift of one eyebrow. The man was totally insufferable. How she could ever have imagined herself in love with him was a complete mystery.

'I can assure you that you don't know me at all,' she told him aridly.

Greg's hard eyes flicked over her beautiful face. 'On the contrary, I think I know you very well,' he drawled smoothly, and then his eyes moved down over the soft curves of her body in a blatant appraisal. 'As well as a man can know a woman.'

Colour rose in her cheeks at the deliberately provocative statement.

He shrugged and reached for the door-handle. 'Anyway, I hope you find happiness,' he concluded briskly. 'My main concern is the happiness of two little girls under my care.'

'Well, at least we are in agreement about something.' She got out of the car and their eyes met across its roof.

'Are we?' he asked stonily, a dark brooding expression on his lean features.

What was that supposed to mean? she wondered angrily as she waited for him to get her luggage from the trunk of the car. Did he think she didn't care about her own sister's children?

She restrained herself from demanding to know what he was implying. The less she spoke to Greg the better, she decided firmly. She was going to have to tread very warily around him and it didn't help to descend to personal levels.

She followed him towards the elevator and they travelled upwards in silence for a moment. 'Will the children be awake?' she asked at last, as curiosity overtook her.

'They shouldn't be.' Greg glanced at his watch. 'They are usually in bed by seven in the evening, but then again, neither has been sleeping well and they are excited about your arrival.'

When the doors of the elevator opened Greg led her into the type of penthouse apartment that she had only ever seen in top, glossy magazines. Its opulence and its beauty took her breath away.

The lounge was decorated in shades of gold and white; it was modern in design and very large, with a black wrought-iron spiral staircase curving down into one corner. The views from the windows were spectacular.

New York was spread in front of her in glittering array. It was just starting to get dark; the sky had turned to a dusky lilac colour and the skyscrapers were dotted with lights like huge Christmas trees illuminated against the sky.

'Make yourself at home.' Greg waved her towards a white leather settee. 'I'll just go and find out where everyone is.'

He didn't have to move far. He had only taken a step towards a door at the far end of the room when it burst open, and two little five-year-olds flung themselves into Abigail's arms.

'Aunty Abbie, it's been awful,' Rachel sobbed as she was held tightly against Abbie. 'Mummy and Daddy aren't coming home any more.'

Abbie met Greg's eyes across the room, and she was glad of the semi-darkness of the room so that he couldn't see the sudden tears that shimmered in her eyes.

She crouched lower down and held the girls as if she would never let them go. 'It's going to be all right,' she whispered as she kissed both of them. 'Everything is going to be all right.'

It was a moment before she noticed that Greg's mother was standing in the doorway watching them. 'Hello, Margaret.' Slowly she straightened.

'Abbie.' The older woman came forward and Abbie was shocked to see how she had aged since she had last seen her. Her brown hair was peppered with grey, and her face seemed hollow somehow, her eyes filled with a deep sadness that just tore at Abigail's heart.

'I'm so sorry, Margaret.' Impulsively Abigail moved to embrace the other woman and for a while they just clung to each other in silent grief.

'Come on, you two.' Greg's voice cut into the atmosphere. 'Let's lighten things up a bit.' He strolled across and picked up the twins, one in each arm, as effortlessly as if they were mere babies instead of two sturdy children. 'For a start-off, you should be in bed. Maybe if you ask Aunty Abbie very nicely, she will come and tuck you in.'

Abbie nodded as the two children looked over at her expectantly.

'Good—now kiss Grandma goodnight and let's go.'

He carried them across and they dutifully kissed their grandmother and wished her goodnight.

'Poor little things,' Margaret whispered in a broken voice as Greg carried them out. 'I still can't believe it.'

Abigail swallowed hard. 'Greg tells me the funeral is tomorrow?'

Margaret nodded and led the way over to sit down on the settee. 'I think we will all feel better when that is over with.'

'Yes. I suppose so.' Privately Abigail wondered if she would ever feel all right again. Although it was a year since she had last seen her sister, she had always been in close contact with her. Her death would leave a terrible void in her life.

Margaret sighed. 'Well, it's good to see you again, Abigail,' she said warmly. 'Even if it is in such terrible circumstances.'

'I just wish I had come over sooner,' Abigail murmured. 'What happened, Margaret? I didn't even know Jenny and Mike were planning a holiday.'

'It was a spur of the moment thing.' Margaret seemed to pull herself together with a tremendous effort. 'It was a weekend break put on by Mike's boss. They weren't going to go only...I offered to look after the girls for them.' For a moment the woman's voice cracked. 'To be honest, Abbie, I can't help blaming myself. If I hadn't insisted... If only I——'

'Come on, Mother.' Greg's deep voice interrupted the conversation as he came back into the room. 'We've been over and over this. You are not to blame. How on earth could you possibly have known that there would be such a terrible car accident?'

He squeezed his mother's shoulder on the way past towards the drinks cabinet. 'Now, how about a stiff drink?' he asked, as he pulled down the cabinet at the other side of the room.

'Not for me.' Margaret shook her head, then looked over at Abbie. 'Are you hungry, dear? Shall I make you something to eat?'

Abbie shook her head. 'Thank you, Margaret, but I had something on the plane.' In actual fact she had barely touched any of the meals on the plane. She seemed to have lost all interest in food recently, and it was starting to show on her already slender figure. 'I'll have a drink, though,' she said, looking over at Greg. 'Brandy, if you have it.'

'I'll make some coffee to go with that.' Margaret got to her feet.

'No, really, Margaret...please don't go to that trouble. I'm fine.'

'Well, if you are sure...' She hesitated and looked at Abbie guiltily. 'Would you think I was very rude if I said I wanted to turn in for the night, Abbie? I'm just exhausted—it's all these early mornings with the girls.'

'No, of course not.' Abbie stood up quickly and kissed Margaret's cheek. 'You go and lie down and don't worry about the girls in the morning. I'll see to them.'

Margaret nodded gratefully and, with a smile at Greg, she left the room.

Silence descended on the room after she had left. Abigail glanced at her watch. 'I'll just pop in and say goodnight to the girls,' she murmured. 'Which is their room, Greg?'

He walked across and put her drink on the coffee-table. 'Second door on the right. Try not to wake them if they are asleep.'

Abigail glared at the man. 'Of course I won't wake them.' Annoyed at his suggestion, she rose stiffly to her feet without thanking him for the drink and left the room. It was clear Greg thought she was as useful around children as a chocolate teapot.

The girls occupied a pretty twin-bedded room. Obviously every effort had been made to make them feel at home, because lots of their toys lined the shelves and a large dolls' house occupied an enviable position by the window, looking out over the lights of the city.

A small night-light sent a warm pink glow over the satin covers of the beds and lent a hint of warmth to the children's skin.

They were nearly asleep, their eyes sleepily drifting as they struggled to stay awake for her.

Abbie sat on the edge of Rachel's bed and bent to kiss her cheek. 'All right, darling?' she whispered softly.

The little girl nodded. 'We are now,' she said in a low voice. 'You will stay, Aunty Abbie? You won't leave us like Mummy and Daddy?'

Abbie shook her head, her eyes glimmering with tears as she looked at the little girls. They were both so like Jennifer—both had large blue eyes and blonde curls. 'Certainly not,' she promised in a husky whisper as she moved to kiss Daisy. 'Now, get some sleep and I'll see you in the morning.'

Daisy nodded and then clutched at her aunt's sleeve. 'Grandma says that Mummy and Daddy are in heaven now. Do you think that's where they have gone?'

For a moment Abigail had difficulty in speaking. Her throat felt tight with suppressed tears. 'Yes, darling, I'm sure that is where they are.'

'Do you think they are happy?' Daisy looked up at her woefully, her eyes clouded, her face bleak.

'Oh, darling!' Abigail put her arms around her niece and cuddled the little body tightly. How did you explain such cruel facts to a five-year-old? How could you explain something you didn't understand yourself? 'I'm sure they miss you as much as you miss them,' she whispered softly. 'I'm sure they are watching over you and they very much want you to be happy.'

For a while she just rocked the little girl helplessly in her arms. When she looked down, the child's eyes were starting to close as she lost the battle against sleep. 'See you in the morning,' Abigail whispered softly as she laid her down and kissed her.

For a moment she just stood in the room watching them, her heart aching. They looked so small, so helpless. Abigail wanted fiercely to make everything better for them, to hold them and protect them from further heartache. She vowed there and then that, whatever it took, she would not let them down. Then she crept silently from the room.

'Are they all right?' Greg asked as she rejoined him in the lounge.

She nodded. 'They are drifting off to sleep now.' She sat down in the chair opposite his and reached for her brandy. Her hand was unsteady as she lifted it to her lips.

For a while there was just silence as Abigail went over and over the grim situation.

She glanced across at Greg and found him watching her closely, a hooded expression in his dark eyes.

What was he thinking? she wondered grimly. Was he as emotionally torn as she was? Somehow it was hard to relate the powerful turmoil that was inside her to him. He gave such an impression of hard control, as if nothing could ruffle him.

She took a deep breath. 'Margaret looks absolutely shattered,' she remarked aloud, glad her voice didn't tremble as much as she had feared.

'She wasn't well before all this.' He sighed. 'Michael was three years younger than me, but even at thirty-two years of age he was still her baby. I think it will take a long time before the pain of losing him starts to dull.'

'It will be a while before any of us gets over this,' Abbie murmured, a look of deep unhappiness on her young face. 'In fact, I find myself wondering if I will ever feel the same again. It's like some aching void has opened up inside me.'

'I know exactly what you mean.' The raw edge to Greg's tone took her by surprise. He tossed back his drink and got up to fix himself another. 'Michael was my brother, but he was also my best friend.' There was such a wealth of emotion in Greg's voice that for a moment Abbie felt overwhelmed by sorrow for his loss as well as for her own. She also felt guilty—guilty for assuming that he was so hard as to be indifferent to everything.

'I always liked Mike. He was a...a good husband and father.' She swallowed hard as a sudden picture of Mike's grinning, good-natured face rose in her mind.

'Are you OK?' Greg looked sharply over at her, yet his voice was gentle, his dark eyes concerned. For some reason the gentleness of his tone made her want to cry.

She nodded and looked down into the amber depths of her drink.

Greg sat opposite her again and for a moment there was silence, but strangely it was a companionable silence now. She glanced up and met his eyes. 'What are we going to do without them, Greg...?' She tried to hide the anguish in her tone but it was still plainly evident.

'All we can do is keep going...' His gaze held hers, a look of deep contemplation on the ruggedly attractive features.

Then she found herself speaking in a low, soft tone...words that she hadn't planned to say to him. 'You know, sometimes when I wake up in the mornings I have this surge of hope. I wonder if it's all been some dreadful nightmare.' Her lips twisted in self-mockery. 'Then I remember that it's really happened and it's like that void opening up inside me again, only wider and deeper.'

It was the first time she had been able to talk openly about her feelings of grief without breaking down. Charles had been very sympathetic, very supportive, but somehow it felt incredibly good to be talking like this to Greg, maybe because she knew now that in their grief at least they were united.

Greg sipped his drink, his face etched in stern lines. 'They say time heals all wounds.' He grated the words rawly and their eyes met across the room. 'We will just have to think of the children now—put their well-being first.'

A wave of relief washed over Abigail. Perhaps the question of the children wasn't going to be as difficult as she had anticipated. At least they both felt the same way.

'I'm so glad that we are in agreement,' she said, a note of heartfelt thanks in her voice. 'I know it will be hard for both you and Margaret to say goodbye to the girls... but you can always visit them on holidays, and England isn't that far away——'

'I beg your pardon?' Greg sat forward in his chair and looked at her as if she had suddenly grown two heads.

'I'm sorry... Perhaps I should start again.' She shook her head, realising that in her eagerness to sort things out she had jumped the gun. 'I think the best thing for the children is for me to take them home to England with me.'

He frowned, then he leaned even further forward in his chair. 'You can think again,' he grated roughly.

'What do you mean?' With difficulty Abigail held his dark piercing gaze, her relief melting like ice in a microwave. She could feel the cold darts of apprehension trickling down her spine.

'Let me spell it out for you.' He almost growled the words, his ruggedly attractive features looking suddenly very grim in the half-light from the table-lamp beside him. 'The girls are staying here in America with me. This is their home and they are not leaving in any circumstances.'

Abigail's breath caught painfully in her throat. With extreme difficulty she pulled her senses into some kind of order. 'Greg, you are not thinking rationally. You can't possibly give the girls the care and attention they need. As you said yourself, you are working long hours. Your mother can't possibly be expected to cope.'

'We'll cope.' Greg finished his drink in one long swallow and then leaned back in his chair. 'The girls are American citizens and they are going to remain as such.'

She glared at him, her large blue eyes shimmering with bewilderment and anger. 'They were living in England up until a year ago...I think they are every bit as English as——'

'No, Abbie.' His voice was hard. 'That's an end to the subject.' He put his glass down on the table next to him. 'They are my brother's children and they are staying with me.'

'And to hell with what's best for them?' She couldn't let the subject drop, even though the ominous darkness of Greg's face should have warned her otherwise.

'I shall decide what's best for them.'

She shook her head. 'No, Greg. I won't have my sister's children raised by a housekeeper or a nanny, which is what will happen if they stay with you. They need me, and——'

'Nobody needs you, Abigail Weston,' he cut across her firmly as he got to his feet. 'Except perhaps that poor idiot back in London. I suggest that the best thing you can do is go back to him, where you belong.'

CHAPTER TWO

SOMEHOW Abigail got through the funeral. She felt as if she had been through the worst day of her life as she stood in the lounge of a hotel passing pleasantries with friends of Jenny and Mike.

'You must be Jenny's sister.' The glamorous young brunette who had been standing by Greg's side throughout the service stopped to talk to her on her way across to the buffet-table.

'That's right, Abigail Weston.' Politely Abbie held her hand out.

'Jayne Carr—I'm Greg's girlfriend.'

For a moment Abigail was taken aback. So Connie was a thing of the past! In retrospect she supposed she shouldn't be surprised; no doubt Greg had cheated on the beautiful Connie, just as he had cheated on her, once too often.

With determination Abbie pulled her mind away from the past and from Connie and concentrated on the woman who stood before her. She was heavily made-up, Abbie noticed, with dark kohl pencil around sparkling almond-shaped eyes. Her hair was very short and sophisticated, her body slender to the point of boy-ishness. 'Jenny and Mike were dear friends,' she continued sadly. 'We are all going to miss them dreadfully.'

'Yes.' Abbie nodded and tried to rack her brain to think if Jenny had ever mentioned this woman's name to her.

Come to think of it Jenny had never mentioned any-thing about Greg's social life. The subject of Greg

Prescott had been delicately handled after Abbie had made it clear to her sister that she was not interested in him—that she was in love with Charles.

As she thought about that little white lie now, she felt guilty. Her sister had been clearly disappointed. 'Darling,' she had said, with that note of deep irritation in her voice, 'you can't possibly prefer Charles... Look, why don't you come over for a holiday and...?'

Swiftly Abbie switched her mind away from that conversation. Jenny had asked her on numerous occasions over the last year to come over to the States, and she had deliberately put the trip off because she didn't want to see Greg. That fact hurt now. She should have come, and to hell with Greg Prescott.

She glanced across the room and met the subject of her thoughts head on, eye to eye.

Greg looked more attractive than ever today. His dark suit sat easily on his broad-shouldered frame. His hair gleamed raven-black in the late afternoon sunlight.

They had hardly spoken a word since that argument last night. In fact, his manner had been downright abrasive. She glanced sharply away from him, but much to her annoyance she could see him making his way across to her out of the corner of her eye. Desperately she tried to ignore him and concentrate on what the woman beside her was saying, but she broke off in mid-sentence as Greg reached her side.

'I see you've met Jayne,' he murmured, putting a rather possessive arm on the woman's shoulder.

'Yes,' Abbie nodded.

'I was just telling her how close I was to Jenny, darling.' The woman smiled up at him. 'I think the poor girl felt a bit lost when she first moved over here with Mike.'

Greg nodded. 'Well, it was very different for her, but she adapted well. I think she was happy in the States.'

'Yes... she told me that she loved it,' Abbie sipped her wine. 'But then again, I think she was determined to fit in because it meant so much to Mike being back at home.' It was strange standing here analysing her sister's life. Dear God, the girl had only been twenty-three. Five years younger than she was. She turned and put her glass of wine on the table beside her. 'Just excuse me a moment,' she said hurriedly, as she turned away and headed towards the ladies' room.

Her heart was pounding and she felt literally nauseous as she splashed some cold water on her face. It took a while for the panic-stricken feelings of grief to subside. She took a couple of deep breaths and then forced herself to repair the damage to her face.

She looked deathly pale and at this precise moment the dark purple of her dress did nothing for her. With a sigh she flicked a brush through her long hair. Jenny and Mike wouldn't want her to feel like this, she told herself briskly. She was going to have to pull herself together and get on with life. She had the children to think of.

When she went back outside a lot of the people who had packed the room were starting to leave. She made her way across to where Margaret was standing by the door, thanking people for coming.

She turned to Abbie as there was a lull in the proceedings. 'I don't know about you, but I will be glad when this is over.' She shook her head sadly. 'I just feel exhausted.'

'I know.' Abigail put her hand over the other woman's. 'You were right about not bringing the children. It would have been too much for them.'

Margaret nodded. 'They are better to be with their friends. I don't think Mike would have wanted them to go through this.'

They were interrupted by some more people giving their condolences and Abbie, after exchanging a few words, let her gaze wander over towards Greg again.

He was still standing with Jayne, apparently deep in conversation with her. The woman was very beautiful, Abbie thought idly. She wondered how serious Greg was about her?

He looked up at that moment and caught her watching him. 'You've left your wine here,' he said, picking up the glass from beside him and holding it out towards her.

Abigail had very little choice but to walk over and take it from him.

'Feeling better?' he asked, his dark eyes raking over her pale countenance as she stood beside him.

'I'm fine,' she said lightly.

'How long are you planning to stay in New York, Abbie?' Jayne asked, as she sipped her wine and eyed her over the crystal rim of her glass.

'My return ticket is for three weeks' time, then I should really be getting back to my work.'

'What do you do?' Jayne asked curiously.

'I'm a commercial artist. I work mostly from home,' she finished, meeting Greg's eye as she spoke. Hopefully he would take the point. She would be much more suited to looking after the girls than he was.

Greg said nothing, nor was there a flicker of any emotion in his deep eyes. It was impossible to tell whether her dig had hit its mark or not.

'How interesting,' Jayne murmured. Then somebody came past who claimed her attention and Abigail found herself momentarily alone with Greg.

'Your girlfriend seems very nice,' she said, more to cover the awkward silence that Jayne's absence had left than anything else.

'She's a fellow-attorney. I work quite closely with her on a lot of cases,' Greg remarked casually.

'Brains as well as beauty,' Abigail remarked lightly.

He ignored that. 'So you have booked your return flight,' he said instead. 'You'll have to tell me the exact date so that I can make the necessary arrangements to drive you to the airport.'

Abigail bit down on the softness of her lower lip. 'Please don't concern yourself about me,' she said stiffly. 'I can easily get a taxi to take us to the airport.'

Obviously that dig did hit its mark because he shook his head and his eyes glittered dangerously. 'Don't push your luck, Abbie,' he muttered under his breath, 'because you will live to regret it.'

A shiver raced down her spine at those words, but she met his eyes with a look of defiance.

'There is no way you are taking the children anywhere,' he assured her in a low growl of a voice. 'For one thing I have their passports, and for another, if you so much as take them down the road without my permission, I'll have you up for abduction so fast those little feet of yours won't touch the ground.'

With those words ringing in her ears, Abigail watched Greg move away from her to speak to someone at the other side of the room.

She glared at his broad-shouldered figure, her heart racing, her mind running in circles. She wasn't going to let this rest, she thought furiously. If she had to fight him through every court in the United States she was going to take those children home with her.

Jayne turned back to her with a smile. 'Sorry about that.' She glanced around for Greg and spotted him across the room talking to another man. 'So what do you think of the Big Apple?' she asked Abbie conversationally.

'Well, I only arrived yesterday. I'll say one thing—the view from Greg's apartment is fabulous.'

'Yes, it's a great place, isn't it.' Jayne helped herself to another glass of wine from the table beside her. 'I'd say you'll find the pace of life here pretty hectic, even compared with London.'

'Maybe,' Abbie nodded. 'I don't go in to the city much any more. I live in Sussex now.'

'I've never been to England,' Jayne said ruefully. 'I've told Greg that when we get some free time he must show me around out there. He knows it quite well, I believe.'

'Yes. He and Mike spent a long holiday going around Europe about six years ago. Then Mike met my sister when they were in London and he decided to stay and marry her.'

'Very romantic,' Jayne smiled.

'Yes, it was.' For a moment Abigail's thoughts drifted to that time. Jenny had been madly in love with Mike from the moment she had first set eyes on him.

'He's the most gorgeous thing on two legs,' Jenny had laughed when she had tried to describe him to Abbie. 'I know you will just love him . . . but not too much. I've arranged for you to meet his brother Greg. He's the one you can fall for.'

Abbie had certainly been captivated by Greg Prescott's good looks; he had been so charming, so smooth, with the most sexy accent.

Both girls had spent a wonderful three months being wined and dined by the brothers during the last stop of their holiday, apart from a four-week trip up to Scotland. They had cancelled that trip so that they could stay longer in London, much to Abbie's and Jenny's delight.

Jenny had danced around their small flat when the phone call had come from Mike saying they weren't going up to Edinburgh after all. 'They are as besotted with us as we are with them.' She had sung the words at the top of her voice. 'Oh, Abbie, I'm so happy.'

Abbie had been happy too, although she had tried to be more cautious than her sister, reminding her that it was only a month before Mike and Greg would go back to the States.

Jenny had pulled a face. 'When people love each other, things work out.'

If only that were true, Abbie thought now... If only Jenny and Mike were here and this was just a family party. She shook her head at the ridiculous thought and tried very hard to concentrate on what Jayne was saying to her.

'Greg is going to have his work cut out with the children,' she was saying now. 'I'd give him a hand if I could, but my career takes up all of my day. I'm as stuck as he is.'

'Yes... Well, I'm sure we will work something out,' Abbie said positively. Then all of a sudden she was struck by a thought that hadn't occurred to her before. 'Jayne,' she said cautiously, 'do you happen to know if Mike and Jenny made a will?'

The girl nodded. 'Oh, yes, I'm sure they did. Greg said something about it the other day.'

Abigail fought down the impulse to ask if she knew what was in it. Her mind raced. Surely Jenny had specified who should look after the children if anything happened to them?

That meant she could pursue custody. She had no doubt whatsoever that her sister would have named her as first choice to look after the children.

Tomorrow, first thing, she would seek legal advice, she thought grimly.

Margaret interrupted their conversation at that moment. 'Abbie, I'm going to leave now,' she said with a wan smile in Jayne's direction. 'I told Mrs Greenwood that I wouldn't be much later than five picking the children up.'

'I'll come with you, Margaret.' Abigail immediately put her drink down. She wanted to be away from this place, from Greg's disturbing presence. She needed some time to think quietly.

'Well, if you're sure.' Margaret turned and indicated to Greg that she wanted a word. 'Abbie and I are going to collect the children now,' she said as he came across.

'All right.' He nodded. 'Unfortunately I can't come straight home. I've got to go back to the office after here.'

'What about dinner?' Margaret asked.

'Don't worry about me,' Greg said smoothly. 'I'll grab something later on.'

And he thinks he will have time to look after two children, Abigail thought angrily, as she followed Margaret out to her car. The man was far too busy with his work and his girlfriend ever to be at home.

Abigail didn't see Greg again that day. She was fully occupied seeing to the girls when she got back to the apartment. Then after dinner Margaret looked completely washed out, and Abigail suggested gently that they all had an early night.

The strange thing was that once Abigail got into the privacy of her bedroom, she didn't feel at all tired.

She had a shower in the *en suite* bathroom and then dried her hair briskly with a towel. She felt less stressed after that, and sat reading in bed for a while, hoping that it would take her mind off things and she would start to feel drowsy.

At midnight she got up and went to check that the girls were all right. They were both fast asleep.

She sat for a while by their beds just watching them. They had been very good today, had faced up to the fact

that it was their parents' funeral with brave little hearts.
Jenny would have been proud of them.

For a moment she found herself remembering the last
time she had seen her sister. She had gone to wave her
and Mike and the girls off at the airport when they had
been on their way to live in America, just a little over a
year ago. There had been tears streaming down her face
that day as she hugged Jenny tightly and said goodbye.

'It won't be forever,' Jenny had said with a sob in her
voice. 'You'll come out and see us, won't you?'

With a sigh, Abbie stood up and crept out of the girls'
room. There wasn't time for regrets—she just had to sort
out the question of the girls.

She noticed as she glanced down the corridor that the
lights were still on in the lounge. Obviously Greg wasn't
home yet. Too busy out drowning his sorrows with Jayne,
she thought bitterly.

Greg had always had an eye for the women, she reflected as she climbed back into bed. He had two-timed
her for a start.

She supposed she had been naïve where Greg was concerned. She had believed the whispered words of en-
dearment, had lived for his kisses . . . his caresses. Yes,
she had been naïve . . . She had actually believed herself
to be in love almost from the first moment she had met
those charismatic eyes across a crowded room.

For a while she allowed her thoughts to drift back to
that time . . .

CHAPTER THREE

ABIGAIL wished she had never allowed herself to get talked into this. She had only ever been on a blind date once before, and that had been an utter disaster.

The memory made her want to leave the crowded room and run as fast as her legs would carry her, back to the sanctuary of her flat. The only thing that stopped her was the knowledge that Jenny would be hurt.

Her sister had talked and talked about her meeting Mike's brother for ages now. Finally she had given in and it had been arranged that they would meet here at this party.

Abigail didn't know anybody and she was feeling more and more apprehensive as the minutes ticked by and one heavy metal tune after another was played at high volume on a powerful CD system, grinding on her already sensitive nerves.

'I wonder where he can be?' Jenny's eyes searched the crowded room anxiously. 'You did tell him nine o'clock, didn't you, Mike?'

Mike grinned. 'Yes, honey. Stop worrying, it's only just gone nine.' Mike turned good-humoured eyes on to Abbie. 'How about a drink?'

'Sorry?' Abigail's mind had been miles away and it was hard to hear above the racket. 'What did you say?'

'How about a drink?'

She shook her head. 'I'm just going to the ladies' room. I won't be long.' Turning, she pushed her way through the crowds. She would give Greg Prescott ten minutes, she decided firmly. If he hadn't arrived by then she would make an excuse and go home.

Abigail took her time upstairs. She brushed her long blonde hair and studied her reflection in the brightly lit mirror with critical eyes.

It was a hot summer evening and she was wearing a white halter-necked dress that emphasised her golden tan and the soft curves of her figure. She found fault with her looks but in actual fact she had a fresh-faced innocent beauty that had already caught the attention of more than one man downstairs.

With a sigh she made her way down to the party again. It was as she fought her way back through the crowds that she saw him.

He was tall, at least a head taller than the people around him, and he had a commanding presence that drew her eyes and held them. When he looked up and she met those dark, charismatic eyes, her heart seemed to miss a beat.

'Wanna dance?' A young man caught her arm as she brushed past, and shouted the words above the din of the music.

She dragged her eyes away from the disturbing stranger and shook her head.

'Oh, come on, one dance.' The man kept hold of her arm. He had hard features that Abigail did not care for.

'No, thank you,' she answered politely. 'I couldn't dance to this, anyway.'

'The next record, then?'

'I doubt very much that it will be any better,' Abigail answered firmly, and tried to prise his fingers from her arm. It wasn't easy—he had an iron grip and he was starting to hurt her. 'Let go of me.' She raised her voice to make sure he heard, but still he held on.

Suddenly a hand stretched over and the man was pulled firmly back from her.

'Beat it,' a tough voice grated.

The man didn't stand around to argue and Abigail wasn't surprised as she tipped her head back and found herself looking up at the handsome stranger who had held her attention a few moments ago.

He grinned at her. 'The jerk had good taste anyway, I'll give him that.'

Abigail tried not to blush. She couldn't believe how gorgeous this man was... If only she wasn't supposed to be meeting Mike's brother, she thought despondently.

'Would you like a drink?' he asked easily now, his eyes drifting over her gentle features with undisguised interest.

'Sorry. I'm supposed to be meeting someone.'

His lips twisted drily. 'So am I... but what the heck? If we leave now they might never be the wiser.'

The words were boldly audacious, spoken arrogantly by a man who was obviously confident of his success with women. But it wasn't the words that made Abigail's senses swim, it was his accent. Although it was hard to hear clearly, she felt almost sure that this man had a trace of an American accent.

'I'm... I'm sure you are joking,' she said after a moment's thought. 'After all, it's not very nice to stand someone up.'

He shrugged. 'I'm sure she won't mind. It's a blind date, anyway.' He grinned. 'They are always a disaster.'

It was Mike's brother. For a moment she almost laughed aloud. Jenny hadn't exaggerated when she had said how attractive he was, but she hadn't told her about his arrogant manner. She supposed that with those looks it was inevitable.

'I'll think up some good excuse to smooth it over to-morrow,' he was saying now.

She shook her head. 'I'm sorry but I couldn't be the cause of such duplicity,' she said primly. 'Anyway, I'm sure you will thank me when you see your date—she's probably stunning.'

He shrugged. 'Honey, I wouldn't be interested now, if she looked like Michelle Pfeiffer,' he said with a gleam of humour in his eyes.

She had to laugh. 'Sorry... but I have to go.' With a casual wave of her hand she turned to jostle her way through the crowd. She was well aware that the man was astonished. He had probably never been turned down in his life before.

'There you are.' Jenny held out an orange juice for her. 'I know you said you didn't want a drink but it's so hot in here.'

'Thanks, Jen.' Abbie took the glass gratefully. The room was getting very hot.

'I don't know where that brother of mine has got to,' Mike said with a frown. 'I'm beginning to wonder if he's coming.'

Abigail shrugged. Would he come over? she wondered. Did she care? He was very sure of himself, very arrogant. He was also too good-looking for any woman's peace of mind. Greg Prescott had danger written all over him.

Even so, when he appeared at Mike's elbow she felt a jolt of pleasure at seeing him again. Greg might be dangerous but he was also magnetically exciting.

'We were just starting to give up on you.' Mike turned with a look of relief on his face. 'Where the hell have you been?'

Greg's gaze met Abigail's, and for a moment amusement sparkled clearly in his dark eyes. 'Talking to a very beautiful woman,' he said drily.

That comment completely threw Mike, who was clearly flustered for a moment before saying, 'Well, meet an even more beautiful one. Abigail, this is my wayward brother Greg.'

Abigail stretched out a hand calmly. 'You can call me Michelle Pfeiffer,' she said evenly.

At first Abigail tried to keep her distance from Greg. She knew full well that he was something of a devil, albeit a charming one where women were concerned, and she had no intention of being another scalp on his bedpost.

As well as that, she kept telling herself that he was only in England for a short while. He had taken three months out to travel before settling back to his career in the States.

Even so, when he took her home at the end of their evenings together and kissed her, it was very hard to remember all those words of warning. There seemed to be a deep chemistry between them. As soon as his lips touched hers she wanted to melt.

As time went by it got harder and harder to pull away from him. He was skilled in the art of seduction and his kisses were passionate, his embrace like melting into heaven. After a while she started kidding herself that she was different, that he was serious about her, and she realised with a sudden jolt that she was falling in love with him.

Of course she had been crazy to get so involved with him, she acknowledged now. But at the time she had turned a blind eye to the possible heartbreak of the situation.

The months flew by and, as the date of his departure loomed closer, their kisses became more and more intense, almost bitter-sweet, their embraces searingly tender.

When the men decided to put off their departure date for another month, Abigail had almost cried with relief. She remembered that evening so clearly now that it was almost like a knife twisting in her heart.

Greg had taken her out for dinner to an intimate little hotel in the country.

They had lingered over coffee, both of them loath to see the end of the evening.

'I'm glad you are staying longer,' Abigail whispered as their eyes met and held across the candle-lit table.

'So am I.' He smiled and reached for her hand. Then gently he lifted it to his lips and kissed the palm, then each finger in turn in a blatantly sensual caress.

Abigail felt a tremor run through her body. All her senses were heightened; she felt almost light-headed with desire as she looked into the darkness of his eyes.

'I'm staying because of you, Abbie,' he whispered. 'I'm falling in love with you, my darling, and I can hardly bear the thought of leaving.'

'Oh, Greg.' She looked away from him and sudden tears of happiness shone in her eyes. In her dreams she had heard those words, but she hadn't dared to let herself hope he would say them.

'Tears?' He brushed a gentle finger under the dark sweep of her lashes as she tried to hide her eyes from him. 'Don't cry, sweetheart. The last thing I want is to upset you.'

'I'm not upset.' Her voice shook slightly as she lifted shimmering eyes to his. 'I love you . . . with all my heart.'

He reached across and cupped her face in an exquisitely tender hand. 'You don't know how happy that makes me,' he rasped huskily.

She smiled shakily. She felt as if they had come to the most momentous moment of her life. 'Where do we go from here?' she whispered.

He smiled. 'We are in a very beautiful country inn.' He lowered his voice. 'And how I've managed to keep my hands off you these past few months is beyond me.'

Nerves spiralled inside her. But she knew she wanted him, she wanted him as she had never wanted anything else in her life before.

She would never forget that night...much as she tried to keep it buried deep inside her, at the oddest moments it came back to haunt her.

The heavy scent of the climbing roses that nodded gently against the open mullioned window. The cool feeling of the linen sheets against her naked skin. The taste of Greg's skin on her lips, the powerful feeling of his hard body against her soft yielding one.

His mouth caressed every inch of her slender body with driving urgency. His caress held undisguised hunger, yet when he took her it was with such gentle tenderness that she could have died there and then with the sheer pleasure of being loved by him. She held him against her fiercely, loving him more than she had thought possible.

'Don't ever leave me,' she whispered softly into the darkness of the night as, sated, they drifted to sleep locked in each other's arms.

As the weeks drifted by their love affair became more and more intense.

'I think Greg will ask you to marry him,' Jenny remarked casually one day.

'I don't know.' Abigail shrugged. They had never discussed the future. Abigail was almost frightened to bring the subject up.

'I've seen the way he looks at you,' Jenny declared confidently. 'Love and passion fairly sizzle in the air between you.'

Abigail merely laughed. She didn't want to tempt fate by being over-confident but she did feel as if things were right between her and Greg. She had made up her mind that he was the man she wanted to spend her whole life with. Whether that life would be spent in England or

the States she didn't care. She would have followed Greg
to the ends of the earth.

Remembering the strength of her feelings for just a
moment, Abigail stirred restlessly between the silken
sheets. She didn't want to think about the past. She didn't
want to remember how passionately Greg had made love
to her. She needed to remember instead his deceit, his
duplicity.

Never for one moment had she suspected that Greg
was already engaged to a woman in the States. The
knowledge had hurt unbearably... Abigail had never
experienced such bitter deceit.

She found out about Connie purely by chance, about
a fortnight before Greg finally left for the States.

They had planned to go out in a foursome that night,
but Greg suddenly rang up to say he couldn't make it,
that he wasn't feeling very well.

Abigail had been disappointed but she hadn't thought
there was anything amiss. When Jenny left with Mike,
she sat alone in the flat and tried to content herself
watching a television programme, but she felt restless
and lonely. It wouldn't be long before Greg went back
to the States; every evening was precious and she hated
to waste one like this.

In the end she dialled his hotel, intending to ask him
if she could go round and keep him company.

When a woman answered the phone, Abigail's im-
mediate thought was that she had been put through to
the wrong room.

'I'm sorry—I wanted room 402,' she said hurriedly.

She had been about to put the phone down when the
husky voice said, 'This is room 402.'

There had been a moment's startled silence before
Abigail said in a strained voice, 'I wanted to speak
to Greg.'

'He's in the shower at the moment,' the woman had said airily. 'I'm his fiancée—can I give him a message?'

Icy cold shock-waves had made it almost impossible to answer. It took all her strength to say huskily, 'No...no message.'

After she had put the phone down Abigail sat in the quiet solitude of her apartment, absolutely shattered.

Up until that moment she had actually believed herself to be in love with Greg Prescott and she had believed the words he had whispered in her ear as they made love. She felt a fool... She felt cheap and used.

It was true to say that no other man had caused her so much anguish so much heartache. She had felt truly let down by him. He had seemed so genuine, so interested in her. It hurt like crazy to know he had only been leading her on, that all the time he was engaged to be married to another woman.

It had been a bitter irony that on that same evening, Jenny came home and announced her engagement to Michael.

'He asked me over dinner.' Jenny's face glowed with happiness. 'Your turn next, Abbie...Greg will pop the question any day.'

'I don't think so.' Abbie had smiled bravely and kissed her sister. 'But I wish you every happiness.'

'Oh, I'll be happy...and so will you.'

Abigail hadn't the heart to put a cloud over her sister's wonderful news with her own gloomy report. So she had merely shrugged. 'You know, Jen, I don't know if Greg is quite my type and I'm not really ready to settle down yet.'

Jenny had looked astounded at those words. They were the first of many lies she was to tell Jenny about her feelings where Greg was concerned.

Apart from wanting to salvage her pride from the situation Abigail hadn't wanted to disillusion Jenny about Greg—after all, Greg would be her brother-in-law soon and what was the point in souring that relationship before it started?

It was a natural reaction for Abigail to want to protect Jenny. Since they were small she had always looked out for her younger sister, and when their parents died and there were just the two of them that bond had grown even stronger.

Still, she had got her own back on Greg in a subtle kind of way, she thought grimly now. For a start, she had let his beautiful fiancée, Connie, know exactly how Greg had been filling in his time since reaching London. It was no wonder the woman had ditched him and gone dashing back to the States.

She didn't regret telling the woman either, she thought now, as she tossed and turned. She deserved to know what kind of a rat her fiancé was. If she was engaged to a man like that she would thank someone for en-lightening her. Her loathing for Greg twisted inside her for a moment. She had that man's measure and she would never forget how he had used her, and she would never forgive him.

She turned and buried her head into the pillows. The sound of a door closing brought her out of her reverie. She glanced at the clock on her bedside table. It was nearing one in the morning. Surely Greg wasn't coming in now at this late hour? Her lips twisted angrily.

The sound of a small whimper coming from next door distracted her thoughts, and immediately she got up and reached for her dressing-gown.

When she got into the girls' room she came to an abrupt halt at the sight that met her eyes. Rachel was awake and crying, but she was being held tenderly in Greg's arms as he tried gently to soothe her tears away.

'Hush, sweetheart,' he murmured as he turned to look at Abbie. 'Look, Aunty Abbie has come to see what's the matter now.'

'I want my mummy, I want my mummy,' the little girl whimpered over and over in a broken little voice until Abigail thought her heart would break.

'Don't cry, Rachel.' She went to sit on the other side of the bed and reached out a hand to stroke the little girl's curls back from her face. 'Mummy wouldn't want you to cry.'

The child tried to stop the deep sobs but her breath caught in painful gasps and she clung tightly to Greg, her face buried against him. Slowly he rocked her backwards and forwards, murmuring gentle endearments.

He was wearing a burgundy silk dressing-gown, Abigail noticed distractedly. So much for thinking he had just come in. Her eyes lingered on his face.

The dim lamplight gave no softness to features that were set in grim lines. As the child's breath caught raggedly, he glanced up and there was an expression in his eyes that startled Abigail. She realised suddenly that Rachel's sobs were cutting through that tough exterior of his, and that he was holding the child with the gentleness of someone who deeply sympathised.

Their eyes met over the little girl's head and Abigail swallowed hard as she was caught rawly in the emotion of the moment. Tears shimmered in her eyes and she looked away, desperately striving for control.

'She'll be all right.' Greg's voice was husky, yet somehow very calm, very much under control. 'You go back to bed, Abbie.'

She bit down on her lip. Was he trying to make a point that she wasn't needed? Watching the scene in front of her, it wasn't hard to imagine that was indeed the case.

She swallowed hard. 'I'd rather stay,' she whispered rawly.

He made no reply, just continued to soothe the child with a gentleness that somehow tore at Abigail's heart just as profoundly as the little girl's tears. After a while Rachel's sobs began to fade and her eyes to close from sheer exhaustion. As sleep started to claim her, Greg moved to put her down. She looked so small and helpless against the wide breadth of his shoulders, her face flushed, her little hands still clutching his dressing-gown.

Slowly he eased her down, then smoothly he took her hands from his shoulder and tucked her under the covers of her bed. She didn't stir, and her eyes were tightly closed. With infinite tenderness he bent to kiss her cheek gently.

Abbie realised in that instant that, no matter what she thought about Greg, it was obvious that he cared for the children. She watched as he tucked Daisy in and then she kissed both of the sleeping children before following him silently from the room.

'Has she been crying long?' Her voice was a strained whisper as they closed the door.

Greg shook his head. 'Luckily I got in there before she woke Daisy.'

'Poor little thing.' Abigail bit down on her lip and for a moment tears sparkled clearly in her bright blue eyes. 'I'd give anything to make everything all right for them again.'

'Wouldn't we all?' Greg raked a hand through dark ruffled hair. 'It's been a hell of a day.' The words were spoken with grim feeling.

She swallowed hard. 'Yes.'

For a moment there was just silence as they both stood in the corridor. Somehow Abigail felt loath to move away from him. It was as if she was frightened to be on her own after the emotional atmosphere in that bedroom.

'Are you all right?'

The softly spoken question made her nerves tingle. She nodded. 'I...I just hated seeing Rachel so upset—it tears me apart.'

He nodded. 'But now that the funeral is behind us we can start trying to pick up the pieces. The girls are young, and youth tends to be remarkably resilient.'

'I suppose so,' she murmured reflectively, then raked a distracted hand through long blonde hair. 'I'll never sleep tonight,' she admitted hollowly. 'My mind is so active—it's whirling around over all sorts of tortuous things.'

'I know what you mean. I can't sleep either.' His eyes flicked over her pale skin. 'Come on, I'll get you a drink.' He turned and led the way into the dining-room and for once she didn't argue with him.

Talking to anyone—even Greg Prescott—was preferable to facing the dark silence of her room in her present state of mind.

She noticed absently that the table in the dining-room was strewn with papers; obviously Greg had been working in here when he heard Rachel cry.

'How long have you been home?' she asked curiously.

'Hours. I was surprised to find everyone in bed.'

Abigail shrugged. 'I think we were all just glad to see the end of today. Your mother looked shattered.'

'Mmm. She hasn't been too well. Really she could do with going back to her own apartment for some peace and quiet, but I'm loath to suggest it in case she thinks she's not welcome here. She has bad arthritis, you know. Usually at this time of year she goes down to Florida for some sun.'

Abigail nodded. Jenny had told her a long time ago that Margaret's health wasn't good. 'Well, now that I'm here there is no reason why she shouldn't go.'

Greg's eyebrow lifted. 'I thought you were going home in a few weeks?' he said, then added drily, 'Children are very demanding you know—very hard work.'

Abigail didn't care for the edge to his tone but right at this moment she didn't have the energy to take him up on it. 'I do realise that,' she said flatly.

'Will coffee do?' Greg held up the glass coffee-pot from the hotplate beside where he had been working. 'It is fresh. I made it a short while ago.'

'Thanks.' She watched silently as he took out a cup and saucer from the sideboard and poured the strong liquid.

'Black, one sugar—right?' he asked.

She nodded, surprised that he should remember. Probably a lucky guess, she decided grimly. Her hand trembled as she reached across to take the cup from him. Her nerves were in chaos. Seeing Rachel so upset had stretched emotional strings inside her even further. She felt as if all the nerve-endings inside her body were being wrenched tighter and tighter and she was hanging on to them with a kind of grim desperation. She couldn't break now, especially in front of Greg.

'It will get better, you know.'

Greg's gentle voice sent her eyes flying to meet his.

'I know I sounded somewhat sarcastic when I spoke yesterday about time healing things—but it does, you know. After a while we will be able to think about Jen and Mike without the pain. We will think of them and remember the good times and be able to smile.'

Abigail stared up at him. It was strange, but something about that low, soothing tone made her want just to fold into his arms. A shiver of apprehension raced down her spine and she glanced quickly away from him. No matter how enormous her grief, she could never let her guard down in front of Greg... No matter how softly

he spoke she must always remember what kind of a man
he was. They were united in their grief—that was all.

She turned away to sit down in one of the large armchairs, curling her feet up under her and sipping her drink
in an attempt to calm the emotional flurry of thoughts.
'I hope to God that you are right,' she muttered dully.
'At the moment even happy memories make me want to
cry.'

He shrugged and came to sit in the chair opposite her.
'Then cry,' he suggested lightly. 'It's all part of the
healing process.'

Abigail's eyes moved with contemplation over his
handsome features. Had Greg Prescott ever cried a tear
in his life? It was hard to imagine. His face held such
determination, such strength. Then suddenly she remembered the tortured look on his face when he had
held Rachel in his arms, and she felt a wave of guilt.
Greg Prescott was many things, but he was not un-
feeling where his family was concerned.

She took another sip of her coffee. Any crying she
had to do would be done in private. She would never
lower any barriers in front of him. She would never lose
control around Greg Prescott again.

'You know... this is a bit like old times.'

That statement sent her gaze winging back to him.

He gave a lop-sided smile. 'I'm referring to us sitting
having a drink, dressed, shall we say, informally.' His
eyes flicked down over the slender lines of her body.

For the first time she was very conscious of her state
of undress. Her hand moved self-consciously to the white
satin material of her dressing-gown, pulling it closer
around her.

He noticed the movement and his lips twisted drily.
'Don't worry, I have no desire to pounce on you,' he
grated sardonically.

She felt her cheeks flush at that remark.

He put his coffee down. 'Apart from anything else, I feel too damned raw inside.'

'It's a good job,' she bit out sharply. 'Because you wouldn't get very far.'

His mouth twisted drily. 'If you say so.'

'I know so.'

'If I remember rightly, you used to be quite responsive—quite hot.' His eyes moved contemplatively over her. 'We had some good times.'

'For heaven's sake, Greg!' She swallowed the rest of her coffee and nearly choked on the hot liquid. 'What we had was a fling, and I would prefer it if you didn't mention it again.' She clattered the cup and saucer down on the table next to her with a very unsteady hand.

'You are probably right.' Although his voice was casual, there was an undercurrent to it that puzzled her.

'Want another coffee?' He got up to pour himself one.

'No, thanks . . . I would never sleep.'

He came and sat down opposite her again. 'You can always think of Charles—I'm sure that will help to soothe you to sleep.'

Abigail glared at him. 'There is no need to be facetious.'

'Was I being facetious?' One dark eyebrow lifted in mock innocence. 'I thought I was making polite conversation.'

'Like hell you were,' she grated impatiently.

He leaned further back in his chair and regarded her with a somewhat bleak expression on his hard features. 'Tell me something,' he asked suddenly. 'When Charles asked you to marry him, did he realise you want to bring the girls to live in England with you?'

Abigail had been in the process of getting to her feet, but when Greg asked that question she sat back, instantly alert. 'Yes, of course he knows.' Her voice became earnest as she strove to convince him that there was no question of the girls being unwanted. 'Charles has told me that he has no objections to the girls living with us. He can offer them a good lifestyle and he is a decent, caring man.'

Greg watched her intently, then his lips twisted in a drily contemptuous way. 'You mean he can afford a full-time nanny while you continue to enjoy yourselves,' he grated harshly.

'That's not what I mean at all.' She glowered at him.

'Oh, come on, Abbie, you and I both know that you are the original good-time girl. I remember you telling me quite categorically that you liked the high life. That settling down was all very well as long as it was with a high-flyer who could show you a good time... How does that equate with looking after two young children?'

Abigail's face burned. She remembered saying those things to him, but she hadn't meant one word of them. Her pride had been hurt and she had lashed out instinctively. She had said those things in the heat of the moment, hoping they would flay Greg's ego; she had never dreamt for one moment they would rebound on her.

'I never realised that you hung so keenly on my every word.' Somehow she managed to keep cool.

He smiled. 'Oh, yes... I remember those words very well. That was the night I really had my eyes opened to your true character.'

'You may have slept with me, Greg, but you don't know the first thing about my character.' Her voice trembled slightly as she spoke but she held his gaze steadily. How dared he judge her on a few words she had flung at him in the heat of the moment? She was not the shallow person he was trying to depict. He was the one who had led her on, he had lied to her, he had cheated her. If anyone was shallow it was him. 'Anyway, as I've already said, I haven't decided definitely if I'll marry Charles—all I can think about right now is the girls.'

'It doesn't matter what you decide. The fact is you can't take the girls.' His expression was remote, his eyes shuttered. Then he just shrugged. 'Anyway, I don't want to argue with you...especially tonight.'

'I don't want to argue either, but I want you to know that I am well aware that Jenny and Mike have left a will,' she answered in a shaking voice.

She hadn't intended to say any of this tonight, she was so bone-weary that it was a real effort, but she felt pushed to the limits by Greg's remarks. 'I'm sure it will name me as the children's legal guardian, so, like it or not, they will come back home with me.'

'You think so, do you?' he drawled lazily.

'I know so,' she muttered positively. 'And first thing tomorrow I shall go and see an attorney.' There, let him stew on that, she thought with a small measure of satisfaction as she started to get to her feet again.

He finished the remainder of his coffee and, instead of looking worried by that statement, he merely gave a short dry laugh. 'I wouldn't waste your money or your time, sweetheart,' he drawled lazily, 'because you don't stand a cat in hell's chance of taking those children anywhere.'

She glared at him through eyes that glimmered the deepest midnight blue. 'Well, you would say that, wouldn't you?' she muttered. 'But once Jenny's will is read——'

'I already know what's in the will,' Greg cut across her sharply. 'Mike told me years ago.'

She stared at him, her heart pounding rapidly. 'And?' she prompted him crossly when he didn't continue immediately.

'And we have been left joint custody of the children,' he grated sardonically. 'Make what you want of that.'

'Joint custody?' Abbie stared at him open-mouthed. 'But that's ludicrous. You're in America, I'm in England...' She trailed off, at a loss of words, her disappointment acute.

'Well, ten out of ten for observation, honey,' he drawled sarcastically.

'Well, I shall take the matter to court,' Abbie blazed furiously. 'And——'

'And the courts will decide they are better off with me,' Greg drawled. 'Number one, I am an American citizen, as are the children. Number two, I can keep them in a very luxurious lifestyle and, number three, it would be cruelty to uproot them away from everything they know here... including their grandma.' He continued calmly. 'I'm telling you, Abbie, if you insist on fighting me I will just wipe the floor with you.'

She didn't say anything for a moment. Her mind was racing through the things he had just said 'OK, you've got more money than I, but that doesn't automatically make you a better parent,' she assured him in a trembling tone. 'The only thing you have said that makes any sense is the fact that the girls would miss their grandma.'

'And Margaret would miss them—it would finish her off,' he said in a dry tone. 'Not that I expect you to give a damn.'

'Of course I give a damn.' She pushed her hand through her hair and glared at him.

'Then drop the subject,' he told her wryly. 'If you don't you will lose all ways around the board. I will make sure of that.'

Her body trembled with alarming intensity as he spoke those words. She knew he wasn't bluffing and she also realised suddenly that what he said was true. She probably didn't stand a cat in hell's chance of being able to take the children out of the country. He was a powerful attorney with all the money and the means of getting what he wanted.

'So are you going to see sense?' he asked, with an arrogant twist of his lips.

At that moment Abigail felt totally helpless and inadequate. Tears sparkled in her eyes as she looked across at him. 'All I can see is a frail old woman who can't be expected to look after the children full-time, and a man who is too busy to take care of them,' she whispered brokenly.

'I've told you I'm going to try and cut down on my workload for a while,' he said grimly.

'For heaven's sake, Greg!' She ground the words out with bitter frustration. 'Please try to be realistic.'

For a second he just looked at her.

Tears sparkled on the paleness of her cheeks and the darkness of her lashes. Her young, vulnerable features pleaded with him in an unguarded moment of earnest appeal. 'Please.' She whispered the word with utter depth of feeling, and for a moment some expression flickered over his harsh countenance, giving her a flicker of hope.

When he spoke, however, her hope sank into the blackness of despair. 'Perhaps I'll get married,' he suggested lightly as he finished his coffee. 'Who knows?'

Abbie felt a cold chill run straight through her at those words. She couldn't bear the thought of some stranger bringing up Jenny's children. It was the most awful thought.

He watched calmly as her face drained of colour.

'So, have you got somebody in mind?' she asked through stiff lips.

'I just might have.'

She swallowed hard. 'Come on, Greg—be sensible. The children would be much better off with me.'

'You and Charles?' His eyes narrowed. 'There is not one chance of that, honey. Not one hope in hell.'

CHAPTER FOUR

ABIGAIL couldn't sleep at all that night. She was haunted by thoughts of the children being alone and unhappy. Thoughts of some stranger not caring for them.

She just couldn't bear the idea that Greg would marry some woman who didn't love the girls, who resented their presence. It wasn't even as if she could keep a close eye on things. She wasn't an American citizen, so she wasn't entitled to stay in the country. She wondered about applying for a green card. She didn't know much about that, except that it took a long time.

At dawn she got out of bed and dressed in a pair of jeans and a jumper to go and make herself a cup of tea.

As she stood in the kitchen and waited for the kettle to boil she went over and over the words Greg had spoken last night.

She was devastated by the knowledge that Jenny had given them joint care of the twins. How could they possibly share the responsibility of the children's upbringing when they lived thousands of miles apart? What had her sister been thinking about?

She probably wouldn't win a custody case either, she thought gloomily for the hundredth time. Greg was a powerful man; he possessed all the expertise and knowledge to flatten her in court.

Then there was the relevant point he had raised about the children being upset about leaving their grandmother. It wasn't even as if they had another grandmother in England. Abigail's parents had died when she and Jenny were in their teens.

'Hello, you're up early.' Greg came in at that moment, his deep voice cutting the silence of the morning and making her jump. 'Couldn't you sleep?' he asked, putting his briefcase down on the kitchen table and opening it to fish out some papers.

'Not really,' she admitted, her voice slightly husky.

His eyes flicked over her, taking in the dark shadows beneath her eyes. 'To be honest, neither did I.'

She didn't know why, but she was ridiculously glad when he said that. It gave her hope that Greg was suffering as much as she was, and perhaps he wasn't thinking clearly where the girls were concerned.

'Would you like a drink?' She moved to switch the coffee-machine on for him.

There was silence as she waited for the machine to boil. Every now and then she flicked a tense glance at him, wondering what kind of mood he was in. Wondering if there was any point in pleading with him again.

He looked attractive in his dark business suit, his hair still slightly damp from the shower, yet there was a look of fatigue on his handsome face.

'Thanks,' he muttered as she put the drink on the table.

She didn't say anything, but turned and poured her tea and then pulled out a chair opposite to him.

Still they didn't speak. Abigail felt her nerves twisting unbearably inside her. Greg took out a gold pen and made some notes on the papers he had taken from his case. 'I'm in court today,' he said casually, as he looked up and caught her watching him. 'I have to make sure I'm well prepared.'

She was only half listening to him, her mind centred on her problems. 'Greg, we need to talk,' she said at last.

One dark eyebrow lifted. 'I thought we were talking,' he said drily.

She frowned. 'You know what I mean—about the children.'

He glanced at his wristwatch. 'I believe I've already made myself clear on that point.'

'Yes.' She took a deep steadying breath. If she was going to get anywhere with this man she was going to have to remain calm. 'But be reasonable, Greg. I'm their aunt and I'm worried about them. I only want what's best for them.'

'And do you still believe that is taking them back to England?'

With difficulty she met his eyes. 'I'm not sure,' she admitted huskily, and watched with a feeling of deep resentment as his lips curved in a half-smile.

He had expected her to back down this morning, she realised grimly. He had played his cards brilliantly and now he thought he had won.

With extreme difficulty she continued in a calm, level tone, 'Surely we can sit down like two mature adults and discuss this—come to some sensible arrangement that would suit us both?' At the back of her mind she wondered if he would help her to get her green card... He was an attorney with a lot of clout, or so Jenny had told her on many occasions. Surely he could sort something out so that she could at least stay somewhere nearby?

He glanced at his wristwatch again. 'Well, I can't discuss it now,' he said as he pushed his chair back. 'I've got to go.'

She watched with a feeling of deep disappointment as he opened his briefcase and tidied away his papers.

'Please, Greg,' she murmured under her breath. 'Please don't be like this.' It took a lot for her to say those words. She was just about desperate enough to say anything right now.

He glanced over at her and for a moment she thought she detected a light of triumph in his dark eyes.

'All right,' he said briskly. 'When I come home this evening we can take off for the weekend to my house in the country. We can talk there.'

Abigail stared at him blankly. She had heard Jenny mention Greg's other house a few times. Apparently it was out in New Hampshire. 'Surely...surely we can talk here just as well as we can at your other house?' she said after a moment. 'I want to sort things out quickly, Greg. I need to——'

'Quite frankly, I don't care what you need,' he cut across her briskly. 'I'm more concerned about what the girls need, and I think a change of scenery for a weekend would do them a world of good. If you want to come, it's all well and good, if not——' he shrugged '—stay here.'

Abigail stared at him helplessly. Obviously Greg wasn't going to make anything easy. He seemed absolutely determined to keep the children and she felt at a complete loss to know what to do.

Margaret walked in at that moment and Greg turned to wish her good morning with a gentleness that was markedly different from the way he had just been speaking to Abigail.

Margaret looked very tired, her face drawn and grey. 'I hardly slept at all,' she said in answer to Abigail's polite enquiry.

Greg's face was concerned as he watched her sit down at the kitchen table. 'I was just saying to Abigail that we should all go out to the country for the weekend,' he suggested softly.

His mother smiled wanly. 'That would be very nice— the girls love it out there.'

Greg smiled. 'Good. Well, I'll be home about seven and we will head straight out.'

Margaret shook her head. 'Actually, Greg, I don't think I'll come. I hope you don't mind, but I just feel I would like some time on my own.'

'Don't you feel well, Margaret?' Abigail went to sit next to the other woman.

'I feel fine... just tired.'

Abigail reached and covered her hand with a re-assuring one. 'You know, if you wanted to go back to your apartment I am very capable of looking after the girls.'

'You mean you are thinking of staying?' Margaret looked at her with an expression of hope in her eyes.

'Well...' Abigail trailed off, not knowing what to say.

'Abigail is talking short-term,' Greg interrupted in a brisk tone.

'Oh...' His mother looked disappointed.

'I dare say I could extend my ticket and stay a while longer,' Abigail said thoughtfully. Obviously Greg wasn't going to agree at this moment to the children's leaving, but maybe given a little more time she could persuade him.

'We'll see how things go,' Greg said firmly.

In other words, he didn't want her to extend her stay, Abigail thought grimly.

'Well, in the meantime I'll take the opportunity to go back to my apartment.' Margaret smiled at Abigail. 'Are you sure you don't mind taking care of the girls? I'll come around and give you a hand, of course.'

'You need to take things easy,' Abbie said firmly. 'I will take full responsibility and very good care of the children.'

'You're a lovely girl, Abbie.' Margaret's eyes filled with sudden tears. 'I don't know what we would do without you.' She wiped an unsteady hand across her face. 'I'm sorry... I'm just so tired.'

'I think you should go back to bed,' Abbie suggested gently.

The other woman nodded. 'I think I will...just for a couple of hours.'

'Well, it looks like you've got what you wanted,' Greg said grimly as his mother left them. 'But just remember that you've got the girls part-time and only for a very very short interlude.'

Abbie glared at him. 'Don't make it sound as if I manipulated any of that. Your mother isn't up to coping with the girls and you know it.'

'Maybe... But quite frankly, I don't think you are either.' He turned for the door. 'Anyway, it's probably working out for the best. I'll give you a day—by that time I'm damned sure that you will be fed up with child-minding and you'll be running back to your lover with your tail between your legs.'

'Don't count on it,' Abigail grated furiously.

He flicked her a sardonic glance over his shoulder. 'Well, you can make a start today by packing the children's clothes for the weekend. I'm afraid you will have no help as it is my housekeeper's day off.'

Abigail glared at the door as it closed firmly behind him. Honestly, the man had a nerve to speak to her like that... And did he really think she was so incapable that she couldn't pack a few articles of clothing?

She got up and cleared away the cups. She was more than capable of looking after her own sister's children, she thought angrily, and she would damn well prove it to him. She cleaned the kitchen with brisk furious movements, her mind on Greg's infuriating assumption that she was some kind of useless bimbo. Then on impulse she turned and made her way into the lounge to draw back the doors and step out into the roof-garden.

The sun was rising in a ball of red-gold fire. It reflected against the glass from the skyscrapers and gave everything a slightly unreal look. It was going to be another beautiful October day, Abigail thought, as she walked to lean on the high parapet at the end of the garden.

For the first time for a while her mind wandered to Charles. Dear, kind Charles—he had seen her through some very troubled times. He had been a friend to her when her heart was breaking over Greg, and more recently he had tried to comfort her over the loss of her sister—had even offered to take the girls on as a ready-made family.

She sighed and raked a troubled hand through the silky length of her hair. What should she do about Charles's proposal? She was extremely fond of him, and he was a true friend. But didn't Charles deserve more than that? a small voice whispered. Didn't he deserve love?

The sun changed from red to bright gold. What was love, anyway? she asked herself quietly. She had imagined herself in love with Greg and that had brought her nothing but heartache. Surely friendship was better than any mind-blowing, heart-stopping unreal sensation? Charles was steady and reliable. He would be good with the girls.

After Greg, she had told herself that she was through with romance for good and she had meant it. There was no way she wanted to open herself up to that kind of hurt ever again. Now, with the added responsibility of the children, it was even more imperative that she didn't make any mistakes...

Greg had been one of the biggest mistakes of her life. She remembered the hurt, the resentment, the need to strike back. No one had ever made her so furiously mad...so deeply hurt.

The day after she had discovered Greg was engaged to another woman, she had sat nursing her wounds and her resentment. She had been furiously angry... so much so that by mid-afternoon she had gone around to his hotel to confront him.

The receptionist had rung upstairs to his room but, instead of Greg answering the phone, it had been picked up by a young woman.

'Mr Prescott is not in, I'm afraid,' the receptionist had told her as he put the phone down. 'But his fiancée is coming down.'

Abigail could remember the awful twisting sensation in her heart. She didn't know whether to walk out or wait and face the woman.

She had paced back across the busy foyer of the Hilton hotel and had hesitated by the doors. In truth, she had only waited for the woman out of intense curiosity; she had never intended to say what she had said.

She remembered the cold feeling as she had watched Connie Davis emerge from the elevator. The woman was stunningly beautiful. Straight dark hair and a figure that any woman would kill for. Abigail remembered everything about that woman.

She had hesitated by the reception desk, her eyes scanning the foyer until she had met Abigail's gaze, then slowly she had walked across to meet her.

'Did you want to see Greg?' she had asked with a lilting American accent.

Abbie had just nodded, then, gathering herself together, she had said coolly, 'It doesn't matter—I'll catch him later.'

The woman had shrugged. 'Who shall I say called?'

Something inside Abigail had just snapped at those words. 'Tell him his girlfriend, Abigail, called,' she had said calmly.

The woman had frowned. 'I'm his fiancée,' she had replied crisply. 'I take it you do know that Greg is engaged?'

'Well, I do now,' Abigail had said coldly, then something inside her had melted as she suddenly felt sorry for the girl. 'I'm sorry. I would never have got involved with him if I had known... Unfortunately, he didn't see fit to be truthful with me.'

There had been a moment's silence. Then the woman had shrugged. 'That's typical of Greg,' she had said in a low, trembling voice. 'I'm afraid this isn't the first time he has deceived me.' The woman had looked away, biting the softness of her lip as her composure seemed to crack slightly. 'He's just a compulsive womaniser. I've tried to overlook his flirting and—well—his indiscretions, because I love him.'

Connie had swept a trembling hand over the smoothness of her skin. 'Anyway, I hope he hasn't hurt you too much,' she had finished shakily. 'He's never serious about anyone except me, he just likes the thrill of the chase.'

'No, he hasn't hurt me.' Abigail's heart had thudded viciously in denial of those words, but she had too much pride to show her hurt.

Connie had nodded, then stepped back. 'If you will excuse me, I have to pack. I'm going straight back to the States tonight.'

It had been the strangest meeting. Connie had been so calm, yet so pained. All Abigail had thought of after that was making Greg pay. She had wanted to strike a blow to his male ego, let him know that she didn't give one damn about him.

She had been furious when he had rung her later that night and calmly asked her out for a drink. The nerve of the man... The moment his fiancée's back was turned he just thought he could pick up where he had left off.

She had told him she had a date, then wished him a cold goodnight and put the phone down.

Later, when Mike had called to take Jenny out to dinner, he had asked her what was going on between her and Greg.

'Nothing,' she had said shortly. 'I'm bored with him, that's all.'

Mike had looked upset at that. 'Come on, honey...you like Greg,' he had murmured smoothly. 'What's going on? Why the sudden change of heart?'

Abigail had been sorely tempted to ask him about Connie, but what was the point? She had seen the woman with her own eyes. What was there to say? Instead she had salved her pride.

'Actually...I'm seeing someone else,' she had announced calmly.

That night, for the first time, she had gone out with Charles.

Charles was a director of a company that used a lot of Abigail's work, consequently she saw a lot of him. He had been asking her out for a long time but she had always refused because of her involvement with Greg. That night she had phoned him and asked him to take her to dinner.

Poor Charles... In a way she had used him. She had bent his ear all night about how much she despised Greg...about what a rat he was. He had listened patiently and had been kindly sympathetic.

'I'm not altogether surprised about him, Abbie,' he had said gravely. 'I didn't like him when you introduced us at the Todmadens' party last month. I thought he was the insincere type.'

'Did you?' Abigail had been startled. 'But you didn't get to speak with him for very long.'

'Long enough,' he said drily. 'I noticed right away that he was one for the ladies. His eyes followed every pretty girl who passed.'

'Did they?' Abigail bit down hard on her lip. She had
felt such a fool. How could she have been so blind...so
wrong about everything? She had always thought herself
to be a good judge of character before this.

Later that evening when she brought Charles back to
her flat for coffee, she had found Greg waiting for her
in the lounge.

'Jenny let me in,' he had said at her look of surprise.
'We need to talk.' Then his eyes had moved over Charles
in a dismissive manner. 'Would you mind leaving us
alone for a while?' he had asked calmly, just a hint of
arrogance in his tone. 'There are a few things I need to
sort out with Abbie.'

'Don't you go anywhere,' Abigail had told Charles
swiftly, as he obligingly started to go. She was blazing
mad at Greg's cool audacity. If he thought he could just
waltz in, murmur a few trite words to her and take up
where he had left off for the week until he left the
country, then he had another thought coming.

'I have nothing to say to you, Greg.' She met his eyes
firmly.

'Don't be ridiculous.' He stood up. 'I think you owe
me more than that.'

'I don't owe you anything,' she said with a bitter smile.
'We've enjoyed a few laughs together but that was all it
was—just a laugh.'

His eyes glittered dangerously at those words.

'Obviously there is no point trying to discuss anything
with you while you're in this mood.' He bit the words
out abrasively as he moved for the door. 'Ring me when
you've calmed down.'

Oh, that man had nerve—tons and tons of arrogant
nerve. Abigail wouldn't have lifted the phone to him if
he were the last man left on earth; she had far too much
pride and too much self-respect to lower herself.

She didn't see him again until Jenny and Mike's wedding, nearly a week later.

Abigail had never seen her sister so happy, so radiant. To her utmost delight Mike had agreed to live in London for a while. They had got themselves a little flat and he was going to start looking for a job as soon as they came back from their honeymoon.

They got married by special licence at a register office so that Greg would be able to attend before he left to go back to the States. It was a simple ceremony, attended by only a few close friends and Margaret, who had flown in from the States.

Abigail had invited Charles, much to her sister's dismay.

'But, Abbie!' she had wailed. 'This will be your last chance to get back together with Greg—he's leaving tomorrow.'

'I don't want to get back with him,' Abigail had replied firmly. 'I'm not interested in him, Jen. I've got Charles in my life now and I'm really keen on him.'

It had been an utter lie . . . but what else could she say to take the hurt look out of Jenny's eyes? The truth of the matter was that she needed Charles there to boost her self-confidence, to show Greg she didn't give a damn.

She needn't have worried. He hardly spoke a word to her either at the service or at the small reception party afterwards. To cover her feelings of depression Abigail flirted outrageously with Charles. She fluttered her eyelashes and laughed at everything even vaguely amusing he uttered.

It was only later that evening when she got back to her lonely flat that her mask of good humour slipped and she cried bitter tears. Jenny was gone and tomorrow Greg would fly back to the States and out of her life forever.

'Good riddance to him,' she muttered fiercely in between bouts of crying and then, in an act of pure bravado, she opened a special bottle of champagne and ran herself a bath.

To hell with the man, she told herself a little while later as she put on her favourite perfume and a very expensive négligé and relaxed on the settee. She didn't need him, she didn't need anybody.

She could still remember the wild feeling of exhilaration when the doorbell rang and Greg's voice sounded loudly in the hallway, demanding to be let in.

Her heart thudding painfully, she rushed to open the door. For two pins she would have fallen back into his arms again at that moment.

The feeling died, however, when she saw the furious look on his face. His eyes narrowed as they ran over the white satin nightgown and matching dressing-gown which clung provocatively to her curving figure, leaving little to the imagination. Then his eyes flicked to the room behind her, lingering on the champagne bottle.

'Well, it looks like your sister was very much mistaken when she suggested you might be a little depressed and lonely tonight,' he grated harshly.

Anger surfaced bitterly as she realised that the only reason he had come round was because Jenny had asked him to.

'I'm busy, Greg. If you've come to say something, then just get to the point.' With great difficulty she kept her voice steady.

For a moment his eyes lingered on the bedroom door at the other side of the room, and she realised that he thought she had someone with her.

'What the hell has got into you, Abbie?' he grated drily. 'Last week we were having a good time together... Why the sudden change?'

Abigail's heart thudded viciously. That was all she had been to him—a good time. The knowledge burned fiercely in her heart.

'Let's just say I'm having a better time now,' she said coldly. 'Charles knows how to treat a woman.'

One eyebrow lifted drily. 'What you mean to say is that you're impressed with the lifestyle he's showing you.'

Abigail glared stonily at him. 'I'm impressed with everything about Charles.'

'But especially his mansion of a house on the banks of the river Thames and his shooting-lodge in Scotland— and let's not forget his Swiss bank account.'

Abigail frowned. She knew Charles was well off and she knew he lived in a nice house, but as for shooting-lodges and Swiss bank accounts... She had never heard him mention those. 'I don't know what you mean.'

He laughed, but it was a harsh, grating sound quite devoid of any real amusement. 'I suppose you didn't read the article on Charles in The Times, then, listing him as one of the country's most eligible men?'

'No, I didn't...' She trailed off in surprise.

'What a coincidence that you suddenly started to see a lot of him just after it was printed.' His voice was brittle with sarcasm.

'Yes, it was a coincidence.' Abigail's voice shook with anger; she was furious at the snide innuendo.

'I'm sure.' His mouth twisted in a contemptuous smile. 'You know, your sister is under the misconception that you are like her—that all you want is to settle down and be happy.'

'I am happy.' Abigail bit the words out briskly. 'I'm sorry if that hurts your ego... but Charles makes me extremely happy.'

He shrugged. 'If I had realised that you were so impressed by money, I would have fluttered it around you a bit more—perhaps that way I would have got you into bed sooner. It certainly worked for Charles.'

Red-hot anger had flooded Abigail's entire body. Without even thinking about it, she swung her hand back and hit him sharply across the cheek. 'How dare you speak to me like that?' Her voice trembled with feeling. 'Yes, I like the high life that Charles shows me. He is also kind and considerate and totally honest with me.'

'You mean he tells you how much interest he makes per month?' Greg put a hand to the redness of his cheek. His manner was ice-cool; that slap might never have taken place for all the impact it seemed to have on him. His temper was perfectly under control as if he didn't give one damn. 'Very commendable, I'm sure,' he drawled now.

'Well, let's just say that if I had to pick someone to settle down with it would be him,' Abigail grated furiously. 'Yes, I adore the parties and the restaurants he takes me to. Why settle for second-best when you can go first-class?'

'Why, indeed?'

For a moment she thought she had succeeded in really wounding his male pride, and she watched his face with a mixture of sadness and intense satisfaction. Unfortunately the latter emotion did not last; it was deluged with waves of deep unhappiness at the bland look of indifference on his features. He really didn't care—that much was obvious.

'Well, I guess there's nothing more to say.' He shrugged lightly. 'I hope you'll be happy with your high-flying friend, Abigail . . . but I've got a feeling that your type is never really happy.'

Her lips tightened. 'Oh, don't worry, I'm sure I'll manage to laugh when you've gone.'

His expression was cold. 'You've got a hell of a lot of growing up to do... You know, I almost feel sorry for Charles.'

'Save your sympathy for someone who needs it,' she suggested drily. 'Perhaps your next girlfriend...'

His lips twisted in a lop-sided smile. 'So long, kid. Maybe I'll see you around some time—after all, we are practically family.'

She just stared into his dark eyes, lost for what to say. All she knew for certain was that she didn't want to say goodbye, even though she knew it was for the best.

With difficulty Abigail dragged her thoughts away from Greg... She was supposed to be thinking about Charles and his proposal, not dragging up past unhappy memories.

But they weren't all unhappy memories, a little voice whispered inside. Sometimes when she lay alone in her bed at nights she remembered the feelings Greg had stirred up inside her; the fireworks in her system when she first saw him; the tingling, wild ecstatic feelings during their courtship. She had felt nothing like that with Charles. Theirs was a sensible relationship based on respect and friendship. Perhaps those were the best reasons for marriage... At least Charles could never hurt her the way Greg had.

With a sigh she turned away from the sunrise. She couldn't think straight any more. She knew she should ring Charles; she owed him the courtesy of a phone call at least, even if she hadn't made up her mind about his proposal. She calculated the time difference and worked out that if she hurried she could catch him before he left his office for lunch.

He was delighted to hear her voice and they talked for a while about her flight and then the funeral, before he asked her when he could expect her home.

'I don't know...' Abigail hesitated. 'There are complications...Greg thinks the girls should stay with him.'

'Maybe he's right,' Charles said briskly. 'It would be an upheaval to bring them to England.'

'Charles!' Abigail was shocked by those words. She expected staunch support from him on the subject of the girls.

'I'm sorry, darling. You know I've already told you that if you want to bring them back it's all right with me,' he said quickly. 'We can hire help and——'

'I don't need help with them.' Abigail cut across him sharply, remembering Greg's words last night about them hiring a nanny. 'Anyway, Charles, I'll have to go.'

'You haven't told me you're missing me,' he said quietly, just a hint of petulance in his tone. 'I know you're upset, Abbie, but don't forget that I love you... I'm thinking about you and I meant what I said about marriage and the girls.'

Abigail immediately felt guilty about snapping at him. 'I...I know... I'm sorry. I'm not really thinking straight these days.'

That at least was the truth, Abbie thought, as she put down the phone. She couldn't seem to think straight about anything. Her mind was clouded with grief over Jenny and Michael and memories of Greg.

She shook her head firmly. Yesterday was gone and she was going to have to pull herself together and sort her life out. The children were her priority. She would have to try and do her best for them.

When she put her head around the girls' door they were just starting to wake. 'Hello, sleepy-heads,' she said gently. 'What would you like for breakfast?'

'Toast,' Daisy declared in a loud voice, and then threw back the covers on her bed to climb out. 'Where's Uncle Greg?' she asked, as she padded across the room to kiss Abigail.

'He's gone to work.'

'Oh!' Her little face fell.

'Will he be gone all day?' Rachel asked pensively.

Abigail's eyes raked over the other little girl. Her eyes were like blue pools in the pallor of her face.

'I'm sure he will be home as soon as he can,' she answered brightly, and ruffled Daisy's blonde curls. 'And in the meantime you've got me and we can have some fun together.' Once more she was struck by how much the children adored their uncle. It made her think again about her plans to take them away to England.

With a sigh she started to organise their showers and then searched for clothes for them to wear.

Although Abigail had helped her sister occasionally with the children when they lived in England, she wasn't really used to organising them and dressing them. A lot of frivolity ensued when she tried to put Rachel's tracksuit on back to front, and then got their shoes mixed up.

When Margaret joined them a little while later at the breakfast table, she remarked on the sound of the children's laughter. 'It's the first time I've heard them laugh since... since the accident.' She smiled at Abbie. 'It's lovely to hear.'

'They were laughing at my dreadful attempts at helping to dress them.'

'You'll get the hang of it.' Margaret reached for the coffee-pot.

She looked a lot better than she had done first thing this morning, Abigail noted with relief.

'Would you like me to help you pack the children's clothes?' she asked now.

Abigail shook her head firmly. 'Thank you, Margaret, but I can manage. More to the point, would you like me to help you with moving your things back to your apartment?'

'No—I haven't brought much, just a small case.'

'Where are you going?' Daisy asked, her small face creased with a frown.

'Grandma needs to go home for a few days for a little rest,' Margaret said gently. 'But in the meantime Uncle Greg is going to take you to his house in the country for the weekend.'

'What about Aunty Abbie?' Rachel asked suddenly. 'Is she coming?'

'Yes, I'm coming—you don't think I'm going to miss out on all the fun, do you?' Abbie answered her with a reassuring smile.

The response to that was ecstatic. Daisy's eyes lit up and even Rachel, who had been withdrawn throughout breakfast, started to chatter about the trip.

'Obviously Greg's idea was a good one,' Abbie said to Margaret later, as she started to clear the breakfast things.

Margaret smiled. 'The girls adore Greg. They also love to go to his other house because he has a dog there and he keeps a few horses. Jenny and Michael took them there a few times...' Her voice trailed off sadly.

Abigail's heart went out to the other woman. 'It will get better, Margaret.' Suddenly she found herself repeating what Greg had said to her last night. 'I'm sure, given time, we will start to come out of this black depression.'

Margaret nodded. 'Now that you're here,' she said gently.

Abigail wondered briefly what Margaret would say if she knew the truth, that she wanted to take the children to England? She imagined that she would be as against the idea as Greg. Guilt made her turn away. She didn't want to hurt Margaret—the woman had suffered enough.

Abigail kept herself very busy that day. Things seemed easier when she kept fully occupied. She packed a small bag with enough items of clothing to last the girls a few days. Then she packed her own, and finally she insisted on packing for Margaret because the older woman just didn't seem up to it.

They all had lunch together and then Greg's mother took a taxi back to her apartment, leaving Abigail alone with the girls.

The afternoon seemed to fly by after that. Abigail busied herself playing with the girls, and then decided to take them out for a walk in the afternoon to give them some fresh air.

It was a lovely day; sunlight dabbled through the autumn rust of the leaves, but it was hardly a relaxing walk. The roads were so busy and the pavements so packed that Abigail kept a tight hold on the children's hands, too frightened to do otherwise.

'Do you like living in New York, girls?' she asked them, as they waited for a pedestrian crossing to change in their favour.

'It's all right.' Rachel shrugged. 'We have a neat apartment and...' Suddenly she trailed off, her little face clouding. 'Well, we did have a neat apartment,' she muttered. 'But we can't live there any more, not without Mummy and Daddy.'

Abigail felt her heart squeeze painfully. 'But you like living at Uncle Greg's apartment?' she forced herself to say cheerfully. 'It's very beautiful and Uncle Greg loves you very much.'

'Yes.' Daisy kicked at an imaginary pebble. 'I like it best when you're with us as well, though... You won't leave us, Aunty Abbie? You won't go back to England?'

Abbie looked down into the child's wide, panic-stricken blue eyes, and hesitated. She didn't want to make promises she couldn't keep, but she did want to reassure the girls.

'I shall see what I can do,' she said with a gentle smile. Then something inside her made her ask gently, 'Perhaps you and Rachel would like to come to England with me?'

Daisy looked up at her aunt, her little face thoughtful. 'Would Uncle Greg come as well?' she asked seriously.

Abigail swallowed hard. 'I don't think so, sweetheart.

'I want us all to be together,' Rachel piped in earnestly, 'just as we are now.'

'OK.' Abigail glossed over the subject quickly. 'It was just a little idea, but we won't think about it now.' She squeezed the little girls hands tightly. 'You know that Uncle Greg and I love you very much,' she said softly. 'And we will do our very very best to make things right for you.'

Then, lightening her tone, she said quickly, 'Now, come on, let's get home and have a nice cup of tea.'

Rachel smiled at that. 'You sound just like Mummy,' she said happily. 'Mummy used to say that.'

Abigail bit down on her lip, her mind racing around in desperate circles. Oh, Jenny, she thought in anguish. What should I do?

CHAPTER FIVE

AS SOON as Abigail had given the twins their dinner she rushed through to her bedroom for a very quick shower and change, ready for the night's journey.

She selected a pair of jeans and a lightweight jumper for travelling, and was just finishing drying her hair when she heard the sound of Greg arriving home and the excited chatter of the children.

With a quick glance at her appearance, she went out to see him. Something made her hesitate in the open doorway to the lounge, her eyes sweeping the scene in front of her with deep contemplation.

The children were both sitting on Greg's knees as he relaxed back in one of the comfortable armchairs. They were both trying to talk to him at the same time and the noise was deafening.

'Steady on.' He placed hands over his ears with a laugh. 'One at a time, please... Rachel, you start.'

'Grandma has gone home—and Auntie Abbie has packed all our bags,' Rachel said excitedly.

'I was going to say that,' Daisy complained loudly.

'Well, never mind, you can tell me something else.' Greg tickled her playfully. 'Are you looking forward to going to the country for the weekend?'

Both girls gave a loud shout of 'Yes!' in between giggling at Greg's tickling.

Abigail moved forward and Greg looked round at her. 'I've just been hearing about your day,' he said pleasantly.

She smiled, but it was rather a wan smile. Watching the way the children seemed to idolise Greg made her feel guilty all over again about her plans to take them away.

'We've had some fun.' Abbie stopped by his chair and ruffled Daisy's hair. 'Haven't we, kids?'

'Yes, we helped Aunty Abbie make dinner,' Daisy said solemnly.

'Well, you gave moral support,' Abbie said hurriedly, in case Greg would think she had allowed them near the hot cooker.

'Would you like some dinner, Greg?' she asked politely. 'I did leave some for you.'

He shook his head, his lips curved in an amused smile. 'No, I'll pass on that tempting offer, thank you.'

Abigail's temper rose slightly at the sarcastic edge to his voice. Obviously Greg thought her completely useless in the kitchen. It was true that when she had been dating him, her one attempt to cook him a meal had ended in disaster. She had burnt a perfectly good steak, she remembered now with embarrassment, but that had been a nervous mistake; she had tried too hard to have everything perfect for him.

'Well, it's your loss.' She turned away from him to tidy away the toys the girls had been playing with earlier. 'We are all packed,' she said over her shoulder, 'so we are ready to go when you are.'

'Good.' He gently lifted the children from his knees. 'I'll just go and have a quick shower. You help Aunty Abbie to put those toys away.'

The children obediently came to do as he asked.

It was only about fifteen minutes later when Greg reappeared.

'That was quick.' Abigail didn't turn to look at him immediately. She was getting the girls' coats from the cloak-room.

'Well, I want to get away before it gets dark,' he said casually. 'Are these all the cases?'

'Yes, there are... just two.' She turned and for a moment his appearance threw her off her stroke. For the first time since she had arrived, he was wearing jeans instead of a business suit. The transformation from business-wear to casual made her remember the Greg she had known in London. He looked ruggedly attractive, the jeans seeming to emphasise the leanness of his hips and the fawn cashmere jumper the width of his shoulders.

He had a fabulous body, she found herself thinking idly, and then her thoughts froze. What on earth was the matter with her? she wondered furiously. She must be going round the twist, thinking about him in that way.

'So, are you all ready?' he asked, one eyebrow lifting quizzically.

'Yes, I said we were.' Her voice held a note of impatience, but it was irritation with herself, not with him. She pushed a hand self-consciously through the thickness of her hair, then bent to pick up the cases.

'Allow me.' Greg also reached for them and their hands met accidentally on the handle of the children's hold-all.

The touch of his skin against hers sent a strange little dart of electric sensation racing through her. Hurriedly she pulled back. 'Sorry,' she muttered hastily.

He smiled at her, and she hoped to heaven that she didn't look as red and flustered as she felt.

What on earth was the matter with her, she wondered furiously? Why on earth was she so jumpy about the mere touch of his hand? Annoyed with herself, she turned to pick up her jacket and then called the children.

'Have we got everything?' Greg distracted her attention as he looked around for more luggage.

'Yes, I just told you——'

'No.' Rachel's voice interrupted them. 'We haven't got Mitzy.'

'Mitzy?' Startled, Abigail glanced down at the little girl.

'Her bunny-rabbit,' Greg informed her. 'Rachel doesn't like to go far without Mitzy. It was a Christmas present from Jenny and Mike last Christmas.'

'Oh!' Flustered, Abigail turned to go and get it.

'It's all right, Abbie.' Greg put a hand on her arm. 'You put your jacket on. I'll get it.'

When Greg came back with the soft toy, Abigail moved to open the front door for him and he shook his head. 'Not that way,' he said with a grin, then nodded to the black spiral staircase at the other side of the room. 'That way,' he told her firmly.

She frowned. 'How on earth . . .?' She trailed off in a puzzled tone as the girls caught hold of her hands.

'Come on, come on,' they giggled. 'It's a surprise.'

'What's a surprise?' Abigail flicked a puzzled glance at Greg as she followed the children up the stairs and then along a little landing towards a door.

'Our other mode of transport,' Greg told Abbie as he unlocked the doors.

The first thing she could see was the blue of the sky and she caught hold of the children by the hands as they stepped out into the fresh air.

They went up a flight of steps immediately facing them, and from there it was like standing on top of the world. They were right up on the flat roof of the building and the view across New York was breathtaking. They could see for miles out across concrete and glass buildings.

'Wow!' Abigail pushed a hand across her face to sweep back her hair as the wind caught it. 'This is what I call a view.'

'Wait until you see it from that baby.' Greg caught her arm and turned her slightly so that she was directly facing a gleaming helicopter.

'A helicopter,' she murmured in surprise. It was a silly comment; obviously it was a helicopter, but she was so taken aback that she didn't know what to say.

Greg moved to store their luggage away in it. 'Well, I wasn't going to drive over the edge of here in my car,' he said drily.

'No...' She shook her head. 'It's just that I've never been up in a helicopter before.'

'You're not frightened, are you?' Greg frowned as if the thought had only just occurred to him.

The thought of taking off out across the dizzying height of the building didn't exactly fill her with delight, but she shook her head bravely. 'I presume you are a good pilot?' she asked instead crisply.

He laughed. 'I'm hardly going to say no, am I?' He turned to look at her, then noticed the pallor of her skin. 'You'll be perfectly safe,' he said in a more serious tone. 'I've taken the children up in her a few times and they love it.'

Certainly the girls were smiling happily at they looked up at her.

'OK?' Greg asked, and then to her surprise reached out a hand to tilt her chin up. 'I wouldn't risk anything happening to my girls,' he murmured in a deep tone. 'Trust me.'

A shiver raced through her at those words. She pulled away from the disturbing touch of his hand and nodded wordlessly, her heart pounding.

'Right, children.' Greg turned away from her briskly. 'Let's get you safely tucked up inside.'

How was it that Greg always made her feel hopelessly inadequate around the children? Abigail wondered, as she watched how efficiently he handled them. It was ob-

vious that the girls trusted him implicitly; there was no
hint of nerves about getting into the helicopter. In no
time at all the two youngsters were strapped into the
back seat of the chopper.

'Right.' Greg turned. 'All we need now is you, and
we can go.'

Trying to quell the feeling of nervousness, Abigail
walked across and allowed Greg to help her up into the
comfortable leather seat, then he leaned across her to
fasten her belt.

She could smell the warm musky scent of him and,
as his hand brushed accidentally across her breast, she
felt her heart jump violently.

He must have felt her stiffen, because he looked up
at her immediately. 'You all right?' he murmured softly.
'Not frightened of flying or anything?'

'No. No, I'll be fine.' The strange thing was that she
found his closeness more unnerving than anything else.
She swallowed hard and looked away from him.

He slid the door closed and walked round to take his
seat beside her.

The children chattered happily behind her, but Abigail
was only half listening as she watched Greg settle himself
beside her and busy himself with the controls. He clicked
a switch and the engine started with a loud whirring noise
that made Abigail glance back at the children
apprehensively.

Rachel and Daisy didn't seem a bit fazed by the sound;
they were busy talking to each other.

It was a strange sensation as the helicopter rose and
then swung out from the relative safety of the roof across
thin air.

Below them the cars looked like small toys on the roads
and the people like little ants. Abigail knew a moment
of sheer terror as she looked down. Then she squeezed
her eyes tightly shut.

She didn't open them again until Greg touched her arm. 'Look at the view,' he urged in a loud voice above the machine. 'Don't look down, look out.'

She didn't really want to, but once she started to look she started to relax. New York spread out before them in dazzling splendour. Sun shone over glass and concrete and the tall majestic buildings looked beautiful from up here. Some, like Greg's building, had roof-gardens at the top, she noticed with interest, and some even had swimming-pools.

'Lovely from up here, isn't it?' Greg said soothingly. 'I love flying over it, especially on a day like today.'

Abbie had to agree that it was fabulous. She relaxed even more as she watched Greg's hands on the controls. He was very capable and his air of total control instilled a lot of confidence into her. She did trust Greg, she realised suddenly, not only with her own life but the girls' as well.

The sun was setting in an orange glow of colour as they left New York City and headed into the purple hue of dusk. For one wild moment life suddenly felt vital again and filled with possibilities.

She closed her eyes and, for the first time for what seemed like ages, she didn't immediately feel that awful cold sensation of grief. She thought about the way Greg handled the children, how they seemed to look up to him with great love. Then she found herself remembering his words: 'I wouldn't risk anything happening to my girls.'

She swallowed hard as a pang of anxiety suddenly hit her. What was she going to do about the girls? How was she to solve the problem of wanting to look after them?

'You all right, Abbie?' His voice broke into her thoughts and she opened her eyes quickly, trying to gather her thoughts.

'Yes...' She hoped she didn't sound as breathless as she felt. 'I'm just a little tired.'

He nodded. 'Well, we won't be much longer.'

She stared ahead into the rapidly falling darkness and listened with a smile as she heard the sound of Daisy's and Rachel's laughter. At least this trip seemed to have taken their minds off things. Greg had been right to suggest it.

'I think you will like New Hampshire,' Greg remarked to her. 'New England is particularly lovely in the fall. The leaves are turning now and the place is a blaze of colour.'

Abigail knew that she would like it. She imagined a lovely little log cabin in the mountains, surrounded by the orange and deep russet of the trees. But the plain fact of the matter was that he could have been taking her to the Arctic and she would have loved that too. The children seemed happy and that was all that mattered.

She must have drifted off to sleep at some point, for the next thing that Abigail knew was the sound of the engine fading into the silence of the night. Her eyes opened wide in fright. Greg's hand touched her arm in a gently reassuring way.

'We're here,' he said softly.

'Here?' She looked around and saw that they were down on a brightly lit landing-strip just below an enormous house which was equally well illuminated against the darkness of the night.

'Home,' he said, looking deep into her eyes.

Abigail's heart missed a beat at those words and she was immediately annoyed and flustered with herself. Of course, Greg didn't mean anything by that—this was his home, that was all he meant.

Greg smiled, then turned to look at the passengers behind them. 'Come on, let's get these children inside;

they are flat out.' He slid open the door beside him and jumped down on to the grass.

Abigail looked round and her eyes moved tenderly over the sleeping children. Daisy and Rachel were leaning their heads against each other. Their cheeks were flushed with a healthy colour, and Mitzy the rabbit was hugged tightly against Rachel's heart.

'Leave all the luggage,' Greg said quickly, as he reached to pick up the children. 'I'll get it later.'

Together they walked across the lawn up towards the house. Abigail couldn't believe the building in front of her. It wasn't the small log cabin of her imagination but a huge colonial mansion with a columned veranda around it.

Abigail had the impression of warmth and light as she stepped into the house. The entrance-hall was vast, and carpeted in a pale buttercup-yellow, with a sweeping staircase that branched halfway up, leading to different sides of the house.

'I think we should get the children directly to bed,' Greg said, heading up the stairs with purposeful steps.

Abigail followed, feeling slightly overawed by the sheer size and elegance of this house. He led her towards a beautiful room with twin beds covered with exquisite Amish patchwork quilts.

'Right, I'll leave you to settle the children into bed while I go and get the luggage.' He put both girls gently down on one bed. They were barely awake now, and they sat looking slightly disorientated as Greg ruffled their hair affectionately before turning away for the door. 'You'll find some extra pyjamas in the top drawer beside the bed,' he said over his shoulder to Abbie.

Organised seemed to be Greg's middle name, she thought grimly, as she started to undress the sleepy children. Organised and bossy. He spoke to her as if she were the hired help. But he was good with the children, a little voice reminded her sternly—almost too good. She was in grim danger of feeling like a spare part around the girls.

Abigail decided against showering the children, and put them straight into their pyjamas. They were too tired to disturb and she didn't want to risk waking them properly in case it was difficult to get them back to sleep.

She was just tucking them in when Greg arrived with the cases.

'I've put you in the room next door,' he whispered. 'I'm just across the hallway, so one of us should hear if the girls cry.'

Abigail nodded. 'Hopefully they will sleep well.' She kissed Rachel and then moved to Daisy. They were already fast asleep again.

Greg stood in the doorway watching her. As she turned towards him she surprised a curious expression on his face. He seemed to be looking at her very strangely as if he was trying to puzzle something out.

'Would you like to come downstairs for a drink or something to eat?' he asked, as their eyes locked.

She hesitated for just a second, then the thought of being completely alone with him made her shake her head. 'No... No, I don't think so, thank you.'

One eyebrow lifted. 'Why, Abbie, anybody would think you were scared of me.' There was a hint of sarcasm in his tone. Then he reached out a hand and turned out the overhead light so that only the night-light lit the room.

'Don't be ridiculous.' Abigail was annoyed to find herself breathless. 'Why would I be nervous of you?'

'Good question,' he said nonchalantly. 'Maybe you think that I might pounce on you, or something?'

'Don't be silly.' She glared at him, her cheeks hot. 'That's an absurd suggestion.'

'If you say so.' His voice was dry. 'The fact remains that every time I come close, you jump like a cat on a hot tin roof.'

Her heart sank; it had been too much to hope that he wouldn't notice. Greg was nothing if not perceptive. She shrugged. 'My nerves are bad, full stop,' she said quietly. 'I can assure you it's not down to your animal magnetism.'

'I never suggested it was.' His lips twisted wryly. 'But you did find me attractive once upon a time. In fact, I can remember you looking into my eyes with adoration when we lay in each other's arms.'

Abigail's heart thudded wildly and her body felt hot with anger and embarrassment. 'You've had so many women in your life that I'm not surprised you get confused between which ones have looked at you adoringly and which contemptuously.' Her voice was calm and steady, belying the turbulent emotions inside her.

His dark gaze was enigmatic. 'I'm not confused or mistaken,' he said with complete certainty. 'And as for the number of women I've had in my life, I wouldn't think you were qualified to pass a remark like that— what would you know about it?'

She shrugged. 'Well, there's Jayne... And what about Connie? I'm sure she must have looked at you adoringly at one time.'

A startled silence fell for just a moment and his eyes narrowed. 'Connie Davis...' he murmured reflectively. 'I haven't heard that name for years. How on earth do you know about her?'

Too late Abigail remembered that she had never admitted her knowledge of the other woman's existence. She shrugged evasively. 'Jenny must have mentioned her.'

'I shouldn't think so...' He trailed off and his dark eyes seemed to look at her with penetrating intensity.

Abigail suddenly felt as if she had skated on to very thin ice. 'Maybe it was Michael,' she said quickly.

'I'm surprised,' he said in a low tone.

'Well, don't be.' Abigail stared up at him and then some perverse part of her nature made her add, 'I was told that you were once engaged to her—that she finished with you because you constantly two-timed her.' There—she met his eyes with a look of triumph, waiting for his answer.

'Michael said that?' Greg's deep voice was cool and level, yet there was a light in his eyes that hinted at deep undercurrents of anger.

She hesitated momentarily, then swallowed her misgivings and nodded. It was untrue. Michael had never discussed Greg's personal life with her and she had never asked. That statement was merely what she surmised had happened. Perhaps it was wrong of her to make it, but she was still curious to know what had really happened between him and Connie.

She waited with baited breath for him to enlighten her, but she waited in vain.

'I think you are mistaken,' he said grimly. 'Michael would never have said that.' He took a step closer to her. 'So who did?'

Just one look at the expression on his face made her realise that the ice had cracked and she was in deep water.

'I really can't remember.' She backed away from him. 'If... if it wasn't Michael, then it must have been Jenny. Someone must have told Jen about Connie.'

'Sounds like a game of Chinese whispers,' he grated roughly. 'You know, spreading gossip can be a very dangerous practice.'

'I don't indulge in gossip.' She stood her ground with difficulty as he came very close.

'I'm very glad to hear it.' He reached out a hand and stroked the side of her face with a gentle touch that made her skin burn. 'And just for the record, I was never engaged to Connie Davis.'

Abigail stared at him, her lips set firmly, her eyes mutinous as they met his. She knew he was lying to her—something he was very good at.

'Anyway,' she changed the subject firmly. 'I'd rather you didn't keep mentioning our...involvement. It's something I have long forgotten.'

'Really?' The word was whispered and then, without warning, Greg lowered his head towards hers.

She tried to take a step back but he caught hold of her arms and moved even closer towards her.

Helplessly she stared up at him, her heart beating wildly against her chest. Her lips felt dry with panic and nervously she moistened them.

He smiled, then very calmly, very coolly, he bent and kissed her.

Shock was Abigail's first reaction. She held herself rigid as his arms curved round her shoulders and the touch of his lips started to deepen.

She wasn't going to respond in any way, she told herself fiercely. How dared he do this? He had no right to touch her.

His lips softened, and moved in a teasing way across the smoothness of her cheek and in against the side of her neck.

She could smell the familiar aroma of his cologne; memories surfaced forcefully as her body was pressed firmly against his.

When his lips moved back to hers, she found herself responding. It was the most incredible feeling. Heat seemed to flood through her. Her lips clung to his and she found herself standing on tiptoe to meet his caresses.

He was the one to pull away, leaving her leaning against him, the sound of her heart thundering in her ears. She lifted her eyes and met his steady gaze. She felt totally bewildered by the emotions inside her.

'You . . . you shouldn't have done that.' Her voice was breathless and very unsteady.

'Why not?' he murmured in a husky undertone. 'I thought it might bring back a few memories. It certainly brought back a few for me.' His lips twisted in an arrogant smile. 'You always were a passionate little thing.'

A rush of red-hot anger replaced the warm feelings inside her, and she pulled away from him. 'And you always were full of yourself,' she snapped. 'For your information, I hated every moment of that kiss.'

'You do surprise me,' he drawled lazily, then placed a finger against his lips as she looked ready to explode. 'Ssh! Don't wake the girls.'

She took a step back from him, her gaze moving over his handsome features and the laughing gleam in his eyes. That kiss had been just a joke to him. How dared he taunt her like that, how dared he touch her. 'I hate you, Greg Prescott . . . I just hate you,' she whispered vehemently.

One dark eyebrow lifted. 'Do you kiss all your enemies so passionately?' he asked calmly.

She bit down on her lip, livid with herself, furious with him. 'Why don't you just go to hell?' she muttered and then, lifting her head proudly, she turned and left the room, trying to ignore the low, taunting sound of his laughter.

CHAPTER SIX

ABIGAIL tossed and turned that night, the memory of Greg's kiss tormenting her. When she finally fell asleep her dreams were an anguished mixture of Jenny and Greg.

She got up at dawn and went to stand next to the window. Her thoughts were confused and, strangely, she felt terribly alone. If only she had her sister to talk to. Her lips twisted in a bitter smile. If Jenny were here there would be no problem.

The sun was just coming up in a ball of red fire, lighting up a view that in ordinary circumstances would have lifted her heart.

Her window looked down over sweeping gardens towards a large lake. The banks of the lake were thickly wooded and the colours of the trees were reflected in the smooth water in a myriad of gold and russet tones. As the sun rose higher the colours changed from muted shades to vibrant tones. Some of the trees were orange-gold and deep, deep red.

For a moment Abigail's thoughts were distracted by such beauty. Jenny must have loved it here, she thought sadly, then with a sigh she turned to have a shower.

She felt a lot better after that, and, dressed in jeans and a cashmere jumper, she crept out into the hall to check on the children.

She was relieved to find them still fast asleep. At least they had enjoyed an undisturbed night's sleep.

Quietly Abigail continued on downstairs to make herself a cup of tea. She halted in the hallway, suddenly remembering that she didn't know where the kitchen was.

Taking a guess, she moved towards the back of the house and, sure enough, the first door she tried led through into an ultra-modern and very beautiful kitchen.

As she crossed to the sink she wondered if she was stepping on someone else's toes, being in here? Maybe Greg had a housekeeper who would not be pleased at her intrusion? She hesitated, and then with a shrug she filled the kettle anyway.

As she stood waiting for it to boil, a sound outside distracted her attention. Curiously she crossed to the back door and stepped out on to the wooden veranda.

The air was cool and fresh, with last lingering traces of an early morning mist. The lawn at the back of the house sloped gently towards the edge of a forest and a small log cabin.

Greg was outside the cabin. He was dressed in jeans and a blue plaid shirt and he was cutting logs with a lethal-looking axe, his strokes swift and sure.

He didn't see her at first. It wasn't until the German shepherd dog who sat beside him turned and ran towards her that he put the axe down and looked over his shoulder.

'Well, good morning,' he said, his eyes sweeping over her lazily. 'I didn't expect to see you up so early.'

'Good morning.' Her voice was stiff as she strove to bury the embarrassing memory of the way he had kissed her last night. Her eyes moved from him to the dog, who stood beneath the veranda barking at her.

'Duke, stop that noise.' Greg's sharp commanding voice rang clearly through the air, and the dog immediately stopped barking but continued to watch her warily.

'Pay no attention to Duke, he's a softie really.' Greg turned his attention back to chopping the logs.

'If you say so,' Abigail murmured apprehensively. 'I was wondering if it was all right for me to make tea?'

He flicked her a dry glance. 'Honey, I was hoping you were going to make more than that. I'm starving.'

'Oh!' Abbie shrugged, surprised by his words. 'Well, if it's not intruding on your housekeeper's domain... You have got a housekeeper, I take it?'

Greg gathered up the pile of wood and then turned to look at her. 'Sorry to disappoint you, sweetheart, but you are on your own.' His voice was vaguely disparaging, as if he expected her to complain.

'That's no problem.' Abigail's voice was brittle. She was tired of his arrogant assumption that she was unable to cope with mundane tasks. 'What do you want for breakfast?'

'I'll leave that to you. You will find the fridge well stocked.'

'Fine.' Abigail turned for the kitchen with a look of determination on her face. Damn man. He was so sure about himself and his assumptions.

She opened the refrigerator and found sausages and bacon, and was in the process of putting them under the grill when she heard the girls.

The back door opened and Greg marched through with a brief look in her direction. 'Carry on with the good work,' he said briskly. 'I'll see to the children.'

Abigail glared at his retreating back, then grudgingly returned to the cooker. Let him struggle with the girls; maybe he would start to get the message that he couldn't cope with them, after a few days of practical experience.

Abigail was just dishing up breakfast when the twins trotted in, looking very cute in matching dungarees. Their faces were shining and clean, their hair tied in neat ponytails.

'Well, don't you look nice?' Abigail stopped what she was doing to give them both a kiss.

'Uncle Greg said that you would make breakfast for Mitzy as well as us,' Rachel said holding up the toy white rabbit. 'He said you could probably manage not to burn a carrot.'

'Did he?' As Greg came into the room he caught the full force of her disapproving look. 'Been impressing the girls with the details of my cooking skills, I hear?' she said in a sugar-sweet tone.

He shrugged, not one whit put out by her obvious annoyance, and then glanced at the plates of food behind her. 'Not bad,' he murmured thoughtfully. 'Not bad at all. Perhaps I was a little unjust.'

'Thanks.' Abigail swallowed down her feelings of resentment as she turned to talk to the twins. 'Come on, you two, let's get you settled at the table. I hope you are going to eat all your breakfast.'

'I'll try,' Rachel said seriously. 'As long as it's not porridge... Mummy always used to make us eat that in the winter.'

'Well, it's not winter yet, so there is no problem,' Greg said quickly, as, for just a second, the child started to look forlorn at the mention of her mother. 'Now come on, everything will be going cold.'

They were walking a tightrope with the girls' emotions, Abigail thought, as she sat down opposite Greg. At the moment they seemed perfectly happy, but it didn't take much to bring the lost, grief-stricken expression back to their faces. She would have done anything to keep that look away from them—to make things right again for them.

Greg glanced across at her and caught the sad expression on her face. Hurriedly she looked away from him and forced a cheerful note to her voice as she spoke to the girls.

Surprisingly, breakfast was a pleasant affair. Although she hated to admit it even to herself, Greg was great with the twins. He made them giggle, and even brought a smile to her lips as he told them stories about the countryside around them.

After the meal Abbie got up to stack the dishwasher and was surprised when Greg came over to help.

'I didn't think successful attorneys knew how to stack dishwashers,' she remarked lightly, as he took the plates from her hand to put them inside the machine.

'You would be surprised what attorneys know about,' he said with a grin.

'Uncle Greg knows everything,' Daisy said seriously behind them.

Abbie met Greg's eyes and she had to laugh. 'The voice of innocence,' she said humorously.

'Quite right, too.' Greg ruffled Daisy's hair.

The day passed by in a glorious whirl of activity. After breakfast they strolled down by the lake and the twins threw sticks for Duke, who retrieved them with boundless energy.

Then later Greg took them round to the stables at the far side of the house. The place was very impressive. Greg owned a lot of thoroughbred horses and it was obviously a great interest of his. The girls were excited as he showed them each horse, and they pleaded with their uncle to let them have a ride.

Abigail watched with a kind of detached interest. She couldn't help it, but her mind was on the way she had responded to Greg's kiss last night. She couldn't believe how she had allowed all those old feelings to surface, how she had just wanted to melt in his arms. Charles had never provoked such a response.

'So what do you think, Abbie?' Greg turned to ask her something and she realised that she hadn't been listening to a word he said.

She looked at him blankly, and thankfully he repeated the question.

'Shall we go down to the paddock and give Rachel and Daisy a quick lesson on how to ride a pony?'

'Sounds like a good idea.' Abigail forced herself to smile as she looked down at the twins.

They led a small black pony down to one of the lower pastures, and Abigail sat on the fence watching as Greg put each of the children in turn on its back and gave them brisk and confident instructions on what to do.

He was good with the children, she thought idly for about the thousandth time. He didn't really need her here at all. The thought made her forlornly sad, and more confused than ever on what was best for the girls. Greg couldn't look after them full-time, she kept telling herself staunchly. He had his work to think of.

She glanced at her watch. She would try and talk to Greg about it again tonight—maybe they could come to some sensible agreement.

It wasn't hard to get the girls to bed that night. They were exhausted from all the fresh air, and could hardly keep their eyes open as they ate the delicious meal that Abigail had carefully prepared for them.

'I think it's up the wooden hill to bed,' Abbie suggested with a smile, as Daisy's head nearly nodded into her chocolate-chip ice-cream.

As Abbie got up to tidy things away, Greg intervened. 'You see to the girls' showers and I'll see to the kitchen.'

Abbie nodded and made to move away from him, but he caught her arm.

'Abbie?'

She turned questioning eyes on him.

'Thanks for a lovely dinner. I'm sorry if I poked fun at your cooking this morning. It certainly wasn't deserved.'

Abigail was stunned by this admission, so much so that she didn't know what to say. She shrugged, feeling embarrassed. 'That's OK.'

Later, as she tucked the girls up in bed, she wondered about those words. It wasn't like Greg to apologise over anything.

'Is Uncle Greg going to tuck us in?' Rachel asked, as Abbie bent to kiss her.

'Yes, I'm sure he will be up in a moment.' Abbie smiled and smoothed the little girl's hair back from her face with a tender hand. 'Did you have a good time today?' she asked softly.

Rachel nodded. 'It was almost like being a family again,' she said quietly.

Abigail could feel tears welling up inside her at those innocent words, and desperately she strove to suppress them. 'I'm glad,' she said quietly. 'Because Uncle Greg and I love you both very much.'

'Like Mummy and Daddy loved us?' The little girl asked anxiously.

Abigail swallowed hard as she looked down into those big sad blue eyes. 'Like Mummy and Daddy.' She kissed the little girl again. 'But you can't measure love, Rachel, and you know, even though Mummy and Daddy are not here, it doesn't mean they have stopped loving you.'

'But they went away.' Rachel's bottom lip trembled.

'Not on purpose, Rachel…never think that. Mummy and Daddy are up in heaven, still watching over you.'

She tucked the blankets more securely around the child. 'Now try to get some sleep,' she whispered, flicking a glance over to Daisy, who was already fast asleep.

As she straightened and turned for the door she came face to face with Greg.

His eyes met hers, taking in the shimmer of tears in her blue eyes and the porcelain paleness of her skin. She knew he had heard that conversation and she looked away from him, feeling uncomfortable and embarrassed.

'Abbie.' His deep voice halted her as she started to head for the door. 'I'd like to speak with you downstairs, if I may?'

Her heart plummeted. She had hoped to retreat to the sanctuary of her room to give herself time to pull herself together.

She nodded and went downstairs to wait for him. It was a bit like waiting for the headmaster, she thought drolly, as she went through to the lounge. She noticed that a log fire was burning brightly in the Jacobean-style fireplace, and a pot of coffee and two china cups sat on a silver tray. It all looked very cosy, but for some reason Abigail still felt apprehensive.

She sat down on the settee and poured some coffee. Maybe Greg wanted to tell her it was all right to take the girls to England? Her heart thudded at that idea. The truth was that she was no longer convinced that it was the best thing to do. The girls were so attached to Greg; it was obvious that taking them away would cause them anguish, and she had no wish to cause them any more unhappiness.

But what was the alternative? It wasn't as if she could stay on in the country to be near them. She was not an American citizen and she would have difficulty staying here... But she couldn't just leave them.

Abigail's mind twisted and worried over the problem until she felt more confused than ever. She just hoped that when Greg came down they could discuss things sensibly—come to some mutually satisfying arrangement.

When he came in, she turned to look at him anxiously. 'Is Rachel asleep?'

He nodded. 'Poor kid was just exhausted.'

She sighed and looked away from him. 'I poured you some coffee. You take it white, don't you?'

'Yep.' He sat down beside her, stretching his long legs out towards the fire.

Silence stretched uncomfortably between them. Abigail wanted to start discussing the children, but somehow she felt loath to be the first to broach the subject.

'You were very good with the girls today,' he said lightly.

She glared at him, her fragile nerves rebelling instantly. 'There is no need to sound quite so surprised.'

He smiled. 'Abigail, you are a constant source of surprise.'

What was that supposed to mean? she wondered drily.

Greg got up to put some more logs on the fire. 'It's going colder at nights now. Another few weeks and we will be into winter.'

'I bet it goes very cold up here,' she said idly, as she watched the flames lap greedily around the wood.

'Yes...but the house is centrally heated. It's not really a problem. In fact, I think you would like it. It's as pretty as a Christmas card around these parts when the snow comes down.'

'Do you spend Christmas up here?'

'Yes.' Greg sat back down beside her. 'Jenny, Mike and the kids joined me last year...it was lovely.'

Abigail nodded. She remembered Jenny telling her about it now. 'You went skiing,' she said, as the memories of Jenny's letter came flooding back.

'If only you had been there,' she had written, 'it would have been perfect. You and Greg, Mike and I and the twins.'

Abigail bit sharply down on her lip.

'Yes.' He stretched out a hand and picked up his coffee-cup. 'You spent Christmas with Charles, I suppose?'

'He took me out for dinner,' she answered guardedly.

'I notice you haven't rung Charles since you've been here,' he remarked abruptly.

She turned to look at him with a frown. 'Is that what you wanted to talk to me about?'

'No, of course not.' His voice was calm and steady.

'Well, anyway, I have phoned Charles,' she said dully. 'I'm sorry I forgot to mention it, but I will of course pay you for the call.'

'I don't want you to pay me for the call,' he said grimly.

'Then why ask?' She turned to look at the fire again. 'Don't you think it would be more advisable for us to discuss the children?'

'That's what I'm leading to.' He sipped his coffee and replaced the cup on the table. 'I was wondering if you had given Charles an answer to his proposal yet?'

Abigail's heart thudded mercilessly hard at that question. She shook her head, her mouth dry, the palms of her hands clammy. 'No...'

'It's just that the more I think about our problems the more I'm starting to think that marriage is a good idea. At least the children will have a balanced home.'

She shot him a startled look. 'Am I to take it you are finally going to agree that the twins would be better with us?'

'Something like that.' His voice was calm and steady.

Abigail was astounded at such a sudden turn-around, but there was another emotion twisting inside her as well...an emotion she couldn't define.

'Are you serious?' Behind the eagerness of her voice, that other emotion ate away at her in torment. Was it a good idea to take the girls away from their beloved Uncle Greg? She hesitated, unsure and very, very frightened. She felt as if she were poised on the edge of a precipice, that one wrong word or movement might tip the balance and send her tumbling down on to hard jagged rocks of unendurable reality.

'Yes, I'm serious.' His voice was cool and level. 'I've had time to think about things and watch you with the girls. I think you had a very valid point when you said that my mother can't be expected to look after them full-time.' He reached calmly for his coffee-cup. 'That's why I've decided to get married.'

'Married?' Abigail's mouth almost fell open. 'But I thought that you meant Charles and I...' She trailed off, totally out of her depth.

'Heavens, no.' He shook his head. 'I've told you...the girls are staying with me.'

She glared at him, her heart racing like some wild creature that had been trapped against her breast. 'Now I know you are crazy,' she muttered vehemently. 'You deliberately led me to believe that the children could come with me——'

'I never said the words.' He put his cup down calmly. 'What I said was: you are right, the girls need a mother as well as a father.'

'So who have you in mind?' Abigail's voice was a hoarse whisper. 'Jayne, I suppose?'

His face showed no emotion as she said those words. He merely shrugged. 'Jayne is clever and beautiful, but as tied up with her career as I am with mine. No... Jayne is more mistress material than wife.'

Abigail felt her face burn at such an outrageous comment. Greg Prescott was totally arrogant, totally chauvinistic. What he needed was a woman who would bring him down a peg or two, she thought furiously.

'You seem very certain that Jayne would have you,' she said scathingly. 'Maybe she would be as revolted by your comments as I am.'

'Maybe.' He shrugged, and for a moment there was a fleeting look of amusement on his tough features.

Abigail reached for her coffee-cup with a trembling hand. She couldn't work Greg out. Was he just teasing her? He couldn't possibly be serious? Nervously she sipped her drink. This conversation was seriously out of line.

'I think your little joke has gone far enough,' she said at last. 'I find your sense of humour totally reprehensible. How you can talk like this when two little girls depend on you for their future happiness . . .' She shook her head, blinking back sudden tears. 'I just don't understand you, Greg.'

Calmly he reached over and took her cup from her hand to place it safely back on the table. 'I'm not thinking of marrying Jayne. It's you I'm thinking of marrying. I think that would solve all our problems.'

She stared at him, completely astounded. 'Surely you are joking?'

'Not at all. As you pointed out to me the other day, it is hardly fair to the children to engage a nanny. Especially right away. They need special care and attention to help them adjust.'

'Yes . . . But getting married . . .' She trailed off, totally at a loss. Her body felt dazed, her mind in chaos.

He shrugged. 'I'm thirty-five. It's probably time I got hitched.'

She swallowed hard. She couldn't believe this coldly calculated proposal—it was like some kind of dream.

'What about the fact that we can't stand the sight of each other? Don't you think that's a big drawback?' She tried very hard to keep the sarcasm from her voice, but it was very difficult.

He frowned, as if thinking over her words. 'I think you are reasonably pretty, slightly infuriating.' He shrugged. 'Sounds like perfect wife material.'

Unlike perfect mistress material, she thought angrily. How dared he analyse her like a piece of meat? The man had a damned nerve!

'Of course, you would have to sign a pre-marital contract,' he went on calmly. 'I'm a very wealthy man, and it would be necessary. Also you would have to sign a contract relinquishing your rights to the girls should we divorce.'

'You've got it all worked out, haven't you?' she said in a coldly contemptuous voice.

His mouth slanted in a wry smile. 'I'm an attorney, honey. I always think things through to their logical conclusion.'

Abigail's heart was beating so loudly that she felt sure he could hear it. She didn't know what to think. One part of her agreed that it would be a good solution for the girls...but marrying Greg Prescott! The very idea gave her palpitations.

'You don't need to answer me now,' he said calmly. 'Take time to think about it.'

'Don't worry, I will.' Abigail glared into his harsh, unfathomable dark eyes. She would have given anything to be able to tell him to go to hell—only the thought of the girls kept her silent.

CHAPTER SEVEN

THE marriage proposal was not mentioned again. It was almost as if it hadn't taken place. But Abigail thought about it; she thought about it a lot.

They flew back to New York the following day, and from then Abigail's days fell into a well-ordered routine. It was decided that the girls should go back to the little nursery school that they had attended before the deaths of their parents.

Greg had surprised her by consulting her about this, and she had agreed with him. It was best to try and make life feel as normal as possible for the children again, and that meant going back to their old routine.

Every morning and every afternoon she dropped them off and collected them, using a yellow cab. Life might feel normal but it would never be the same, Abigail thought, as she stood outside the nursery waiting for them.

The strange thing was that Abigail was starting to enjoy the pattern of her days. She liked the inconsequential chatter over the breakfast-table with Greg and the twins. She liked the way the girls ran out of school and flung themselves into her arms as if they hadn't seen her for a week. She liked the evenings, when they laughed in the shower and asked for stories before going to sleep. Greg was always home in time for the children's bedtime. The twins wouldn't go to sleep until he had come in and tucked them up.

Then, there was just her and Greg. Sometimes Greg did paperwork, sometimes they watched a film together or read. The atmosphere was tranquil and Abigail felt it was just what she needed after so much emotional turmoil.

It was over two weeks now since Abigail had arrived in the States, and yet England felt like another lifetime away. Soon she would have to make a judgement that could affect the rest of her life: whether to stay or go home. Abruptly she turned her mind away from that, afraid of that decision.

She glanced at her watch. Any moment now the school doors would burst open and Daisy and Rachel would be running towards her as fast as their little legs would carry them.

'Abigail?' The sound of Greg's deep voice made her whirl round.

'What on earth are you doing here?' she asked in surprise.

One eyebrow lifted. 'That's hardly the best of welcomes,' he said drily.

'Sorry, it's just that you've taken me by surprise. You don't usually manage to finish work in time to pick the girls up.'

'It just so happens that, by making a supreme effort, I've managed it today,' he said with a grin, then waved towards the Mercedes parked behind him. 'My chariot awaits you.'

Abigail laughed. 'Well, I'm pleased to see you. I must admit it's very cold today.'

'Yes.' His eyes raked over the black jacket and ski-pants that she wore. 'If you are thinking of staying on, we will have to get you some warmer clothes.'

Abigail felt her cheeks burn at those words. It was the first time he had referred to her staying. She had almost started to wonder if she had dreamt that astonishing marriage proposal.

'Well, I can get my own clothes.' She turned away from him to look once more towards the school door.

'Does that mean you are contemplating saying yes?' he asked softly.

Abigail flicked him a sideways glance. 'I really don't think this is the time or place to discuss this,' she said in a low tone. For the first time she noticed the interested looks Greg was receiving from the other mothers who stood waiting for their children.

She had to admit that he did look very handsome. He wore a long dark overcoat that seemed to emphasise the black sheen of his hair and the broad powerful build of his body.

'OK,' he said easily. 'So how about dinner tonight?'

'Dinner?' She turned to look at him fully, totally taken aback by the invitation.

'Yes, dinner—that thing you eat with a knife and fork,' he said, with a wry grin.

'You mean, go out?' She tried to qualify the invitation, frightened of misunderstanding him. Was Greg suggesting a date?

'Yes, out,' he said patiently. 'I'll take you to a good restaurant. It's the least I can do after all the meals you've cooked for me recently.'

'There is really no need,' she said quickly, with a shake of her head. 'And, anyway, who will look after the children?'

'My housekeeper.' He reached out a hand and touched her cheek. 'Alison is more than capable of watching them for a few hours and the children are fond of her.'

She hesitated, very unsure of what to say.

'Come on, Abbie. Just a couple of hours.' He reached out a hand and touched her face again. 'We need to talk.' The softness of his voice and the gentle touch of his warm hand against the chill of her face made her shiver violently. She pulled abruptly away from him, and as she did so she noticed the dark expression in his eyes.

The school doors opened at that moment and a crowd of youngsters spilled out into the yard. There was no time after that for private conversations.

Daisy and Rachel squealed with delight when they saw Greg. They flung themselves into his arms and he lifted them high and twirled them around so that they laughed with delight.

'Now, that's what I call a welcome,' he said, as he planted a kiss on each of their cheeks and put them down.

'Did you have a good day at school?' Abbie asked as she kissed them, and held their hands as they walked towards Greg's car.

'Yes, we drew pictures,' Daisy said with great importance.

'Is that so?' Greg sounded impressed as he opened the doors of the car. 'You'll have to show us when we get home.'

It took a few minutes to make sure the children were safely strapped in the back with their seatbelts, then Abbie climbed into the passenger seat beside Greg.

The traffic was hectic as usual and the journey was full of hold-ups. Daisy, impatient as always, started to open her school-bag. 'I'll show you those paintings now,' she said solemnly.

Abigail turned in her seat and watched as the little girl fished two sheets of paper from her satchel.

'That's Rachel's picture.' She handed it over and waited for Abigail's comments.

'Very good.' Abbie nodded approval of the colourful smudges that represented Mitzy the rabbit. 'What do you think, Greg?' She held it up for him to give it a quick glance.

'Very artistic,' he said with a grin.

'Mine is better.' Daisy handed the next sheet over to her aunt. 'It's of Mummy and Daddy in heaven.'

Abigail's hand trembled slightly as she took the paper from the little girl. 'What are they doing?' she asked with a frown, as she tried to define the two blurbs of colour.

'Kissing, silly.'

'Kissing...?' Abigail was momentarily at a loss for what to say to that.

'Well, Mummy and Daddy used to kiss,' Daisy said earnestly. 'And I thought maybe they might still kiss in heaven.'

Abigail's eyes brimmed with sudden tears. 'It's beautiful, Daisy,' she said huskily as she handed the picture back.

For a moment she had to fight the sudden over-whelming grief building up inside her, and she couldn't speak for fear of breaking down.

Greg's hand moved from the steering-wheel and covered hers with a gentle reassuring pressure. 'That was a lovely idea, Daisy,' he said gently.

'Do you and Aunty Abbie ever kiss?' the child asked suddenly. 'Because I could paint you next time.'

Abigail tried to smile through her tears at such simple innocence.

Greg laughed softly and then, as they pulled to a halt at the next set of traffic-lights, he suddenly reached across and swiftly kissed Abigail on the lips. 'How's that?' he said playfully. 'Can we expect another masterpiece next week?'

Abigail was barely listening to the exchange. Her body was shaking inside. The softness of Greg's kiss had un-leashed a multitude of emotions inside her. Incredibly, she desperately wanted to be held by him, cradled in those strong arms and sheltered from the trauma inside.

He had just caught her at a vulnerable time, she told herself stiffly, and the kiss had been so quick that it couldn't possibly have stirred any feelings of longing inside her.

Abigail was very grateful after that when the conversation returned to the normal subject of what was for dinner.

'Rachel's favourite. Chicken and French fries.' Abigail's voice wasn't completely steady, but she controlled it with iron will-power.

'But Aunty Abbie and I might go out for dinner tonight,' Greg said smoothly.

Abbie knew that was her cue either to accept the invitation or say something to get out of it.

He flashed her an inquisitive look. 'Shall I book a table for eight o'clock?'

She hesitated, and then shook her head. She didn't want to leave the girls, even for a few hours. Their little minds were still so bewildered and defenceless—she couldn't bear it if they were to cry out for her and she wasn't there.

'Let's eat in, Greg,' she said quickly. 'I'll make something special.'

He looked startled. 'I'm offering the best restaurant in town,' he said crisply. 'Excellent cuisine——'

'I'm sorry if my cuisine isn't up to standard,' she cut in with irritation. 'But I don't want to go out.'

'I didn't mean to suggest——'

'Please, Greg.' She cut across his patient tone and turned shimmering eyes on him, before dropping her tone a few decibels so that the children couldn't hear over their chatter. 'I don't want to leave the girls, even for a few hours.'

A flicker of surprise showed in his dark eyes but he nodded. 'OK, but I insist on doing dinner for us.'

She shrugged. 'I don't mind cooking——'

'I know.' It was his turn to interrupt her now. 'But I insist.' He grinned good-naturedly. 'You see to the girls' tea and I'll see to our dinner. Deal?'

She hesitated. Usually they ate with the girls, but why not? she thought rationally. After all, they needed to talk, and over dinner was probably a good time. She nodded. 'Deal,' she said softly.

'How are things going?' After tucking the girls up in bed, Abigail couldn't resist going through to the kitchen to see if she could give Greg a hand.

He met her at the door. 'Out,' he said firmly.

'But I don't mind giving you a hand.' She tried to look over his shoulder to see what was cooking, but he was too tall.

'Don't be so nosy,' he said with a grin. 'What's the matter? Don't you think I can cook?'

She had to smile at that. 'Come to think of it, no,' she said cheekily.

He gave her a stern look, but laughter glittered in his eyes. 'Go and make yourself beautiful or something.'

'Am I not beautiful already?' It was just a teasing remark made off the cuff, but once she had said the words she regretted them. Now he would think she was fishing for compliments.

The laughter faded out of his expression and his dark eyes moved over the softness of her skin, which was heightened by embarrassed colour. 'Well...' he drawled lazily.

'You don't have to answer that,' she put in hurriedly. 'I was joking, Greg.' She started to turn away from him but he caught hold of her arm.

'I'd like to answer,' he said in a low husky tone that did strange things to her pulse-rate. 'I think you are a very beautiful woman.'

She couldn't bring herself to look at him. Her heart was pounding uncomfortably and her face felt red-hot. 'Thank you,' she said stiffly.

'You're welcome.' The humour was back in his voice as he let go of her arm.

'I'll leave you to it, anyway.' She mumbled the words and hurried away towards her bedroom, feeling foolish in the extreme.

'Stupid, really stupid.' She murmured the words as she closed her bedroom door and leaned back against it. What on earth had possessed her to say something like that?

She took a few deep breaths, willing herself just to forget it. It was trivial, and Greg probably wouldn't give it a second thought.

Even so, as she went through to her bathroom and ran the shower, her mind went back to the husky note in his voice when he had told her she was beautiful.

Really annoyed with herself, she stripped off and stood under the forceful jet of water. Greg was probably well practised at putting the right note into his voice when he told a woman he found her attractive. If he was serious about his suggestion of marriage, then he probably felt obliged to be complimentary.

Did he also feel obliged to lie to her about the past? she wondered suddenly. It nagged at the back of her mind that he had been less than truthful about his engagement with Connie. Why lie after all these years? she wondered angrily. Was he just a compulsive liar? Somehow those words didn't seem to fit the man she had come to know over these last few weeks.

He was so good with the girls, so tender and caring. He had also been very considerate towards her over these last few days, she admitted grudgingly. His manner had been gentle and sometimes, like today, when grief had overcome her, he had reached to touch her with a comforting hand. She had to admit that, much as she distrusted him, his presence over this last bleak period had been comforting.

She stepped out of the shower and dried herself briskly. Even so, she wouldn't be blinded by outward appearances, she told herself firmly. She had misread the signals once before with disastrous consequences.

She flicked through her wardrobe, searching for something suitable to put on, but her mind wasn't tuned in to the meagre selection of clothes. She was wondering what she should say to Greg if he asked her again about marriage?

She took out a plain black dress, and then crossed to her dressing-table to dry her hair. Her movements were almost automatic, her mind in complete turmoil.

She ran through the options again and again. Then she remembered little things the girls had said. Poignant things that told her clearly what they hoped for in their little hearts. They wanted both her and their Uncle Greg to be with them . . . that much was obvious.

'Oh, God, what should I do?' She buried her head in her hands for a moment, as the momentous pressure of making the right decision seemed unbearable.

As a young girl she had dreamt of marrying for love, of some handsome man whisking her off her feet, telling her he loved her more than life itself.

Her lips twisted at the naïve sentiment. She had certainly grown up since then.

With a sigh, she brushed the gleaming length of her long blonde hair. Only one thing was certain: she did love the girls and they loved her. A life without them seemed somehow unbearable.

With trembling hands she pulled the black velvet dress on and, with a brief glance at her appearance, turned to go and face Greg.

When she went through to the dining-room she was surprised to see the table beautifully laid. Candlelight flickered over silver and crystal. The lights were low, giving emphasis to the intimacy of the table and the panoramic view of the glittering New York lights against the velvet darkness of the night sky.

For a moment Abigail stood by the window, her attention held by the beauty of the city by night. Had Jenny been happy in New York? she wondered absently. It was hard to tell from letters, certainly she had always expressed a love for the States. But had she been homesick?

'What would you like to drink, Abbie?' Greg's voice made her whirl nervously round.

'Just Perrier, if you have it.' As she spoke, her eyes glanced over his appearance. He had changed into a dark blue suit, and his dark hair, swept back from the hard-boned, handsome face, sat in neat precision.

'Everything is under control in the kitchen, I take it?' she asked lightly.

He grinned. 'Actually, I have a confession to make.' He turned to pour her a glass of sparkling water from the drinks cabinet behind him.

'Yes?' She frowned as he didn't immediately enlighten her.

He turned and handed her the drink. 'I had it catered.'

'Catered?'

'I decided if Mohammed won't go to the mountain, I'd bring the mountain in.' He waved her towards a seat at the table and then handed her a menu. 'I hope I've chosen well?'

Abigail's eyes flicked over the list of delicious food, noting that he had chosen a lot of things that were her favourites. Obviously a fluke, she thought grimly. He couldn't possibly remember such details.

'Not bad,' she said quietly, and placed the menu down. 'But you shouldn't have gone to so much trouble.' In actual fact she wasn't that hungry; her appetite seemed to have deserted her over these last weeks and she had lost even more weight.

'It wasn't any trouble.' He lifted the covers on some silver serving dishes and placed a starter of smoked salmon in front of her.

She toyed with her glass, waiting for him to take the seat opposite before picking up her knife and fork.

Why was he doing this? she wondered. There was no need for candlelight or the soft music that was now filtering through the music system. They both knew they were here together out of necessity—the whole thing was a charade. She toyed with the food in front of her, waiting for him to get to the point.

'Do eat something, Abbie,' he said gently. 'You've hardly eaten enough to keep a bird alive over these last few weeks.'

She shot him a startled glance, surprised he had been bothered to notice.

'Starving yourself isn't going to help the girls,' he added seriously.

'No.' She tried to force herself to eat a few mouthfuls of the delicious fish. He was right; she couldn't afford to get sick. She needed all her strength to get them through this rough period.

'Did you look in on them?' she asked suddenly. 'They were waiting for you——'

'Yes, of course,' he interrupted smoothly. 'I tucked them in and dimmed the lights for them. They were asleep before I was out of the door.'

'They were tired.' She nodded, then sighed. 'I worry about them so much, Greg. I mean, what must be going through their little minds?' For a moment there was an unguarded note of anguish in her voice. 'That picture, for instance? What was in Daisy's mind when she drew it? Do you think she's all right? Do you think we need professional counselling for them?'

'An analyst, you mean?' he asked drily, and then shook his head. 'I think it will take a while for them to adjust,' he said easily. 'They need plenty of love and reassurance, and you are giving them that.' He reached across and filled the glass next to her water with wine.

'As for that picture, I think it's only natural that they should wonder about their parents and fret about them. At least the picture was a happy one. Maybe it shows Daisy is adjusting and is thinking about her mum and dad in a happy way.'

'Maybe.' She wasn't totally convinced.

'You'll be the one needing professional help if you don't eat something,' he declared briskly.

She smiled wanly. 'You sound almost as if you give a damn.'

He frowned at that. 'I know I'm not your number one favourite person,' he grated harshly. 'But I'm not completely without feelings. Of course I give a damn.'

'I'm sorry.' She looked away from him, out at the skyline of Manhattan. 'That comment was unnecessary.'

He sighed. 'I know you are unhappy, Abbie. I know you miss your sister. But we have to collect our thoughts, we have to concentrate on the future.'

'Yes.' She forced a bright smile to her lips, trying to belie the tears she knew were not far away. 'But I do miss her, Greg.' For a moment her voice broke. 'Oh, I'm so sorry.' She waved him down as he started to rise to his feet. 'Sometimes I'm fine and then other times I feel as if I'm in the middle of some terrible storm, torn between grief and the need to carry on.'

'I know.' His eyes were full of concern as they moved over the pallor of her face. 'But you're not alone, Abbie. I think we are riding this particular storm together, and together we will get through it.'

She didn't know how to answer that, so she just stared at him wordlessly. Was that a prelude to asking her to stay?

Then slowly he reached across and raised her hand to his lips, pressing a kiss against its palm. The caress was so reminiscent of that night so long ago, when she had first given herself to him, that her breathing seemed to freeze in her chest.

'Don't.' Abruptly she pulled her hand away from him as if she had been burnt. 'Don't, Greg...don't touch me.'

For a moment there was a tense silence. Then he shrugged. 'I think it's decision time, Abbie,' he said in a strained tone. 'What do you want to do? Stay here with me and the girls or go back to Charles?'

'Between the devil and the deep blue sea,' she murmured numbly. 'I can't believe how clinical you can be.'

There was a remote harshness on Greg's countenance for a moment. 'My first priority is to my brother's children. I thought you felt the same.'

'I do feel the same,' she said softly. 'You know I do. But marriage...' She trailed off, at a complete loss. 'It seems such a preposterous idea.' She muttered the words almost to herself. 'A marriage that isn't based on love isn't really a marriage... How can it be?' She looked up at him, her eyes shimmering with uncertainty, her skin so pale that it almost looked translucent.

'Poor darling.' He touched her cheek with a gentle finger. 'That is a very naïve statement.'

Her eyes clouded. 'I don't think so. Love is what makes the world go around...or haven't you heard?'

To her annoyance, he just laughed at that. 'Love can also tear your world apart—haven't you heard that?' He got up and took her plate away from her, then replaced it with her main course.

They didn't speak again until he took his seat opposite. 'It may interest you to know, Abigail, that a lot of arranged marriages are very successful. In some cases the couple in question haven't even met each other before they exchange their vows.'

She looked away from him. 'Well, that is taking a hell of a risk, to my mind.'

'Marriage is a risk,' he grated sardonically. 'Love isn't a magic word you can conjure up to protect you from risk.'

'No, but it's a good start,' she maintained stubbornly.

'So is friendship and respect,' he said levelly.

She glanced down at the food in front of her. Although it was attractively presented, and certainly looked delicious, she had no interest in it.

'If you are worried about finances, then I should tell you that I'm very well placed,' he continued drily. 'The girls will have the best of educations, and you——'

'For heaven's sake, Greg, I really couldn't give a damn about how much money you have.' She ground the words out bitterly.

'No...I'm beginning to realise that.' He seemed about to say something else, then shrugged. 'Is it Charles? Are you deeply in love with him?'

She reached for her wine glass. 'I don't think that's any of your business,' she said shakily.

Was she even a little bit in love with Charles? she asked herself warily. She was fond of him, but she couldn't honestly say that she was. She glanced across at Greg, her eyes moving over the rugged planes of his face and lingering for a moment on the sensuous curve of his lips.

She put a shaky hand to her face, cursing her emotional state, desperately trying to think straight. 'I don't even know what kind of marriage you want.' Her blue eyes locked with the piercing darkness of his. 'I...I mean is it a short-term thing? Is it...is it purely in name only?' She forced herself to ask the question that had been at the back of her mind from the moment he first suggested marriage.

'Oh, no.' His mouth set in a determined line. 'I certainly don't intend to have a marriage that's in name only.' He leaned back in his chair, his manner totally composed. 'I'm a red-blooded male, Abbie...you should know that. A marriage that doesn't involve lovemaking would not suit me at all.'

Her face flamed at those blatant words. 'Lovemaking without the love?' she whispered, with a shake of her head. 'It sounds incongruous.'

His eyes hardened. 'Would you prefer me to call it sex?'

Her eyes fell from his and her heart lurched as if he had just pushed a wooden stake through it.

He leaned forward. 'Don't be foolish, Abbie. You are clouding your mind with emotional issues—think with your head. Think what it will mean for the girls.'

She lifted her eyes slowly back to his. The pain in them was clearly evident, she knew that, but she was unable to mask it.

For a moment his mouth tightened and there was an expression on his lean, handsome features that looked almost bleak. 'I know in ordinary circumstances it is not what you would have chosen,' he said in a cool, clipped tone.

'No, it's not.' Her voice quivered just for a moment before she gathered herself together. 'But you are right— it is important to think of the girls first.'

For a second the light of triumph entered the darkness of his eyes. Then he reached into the pocket of his jacket and took out a small box. 'Would you like to try this on for size?'

She took the box with trembling fingers and lifted the lid.

Inside, a gold band inlaid with diamonds sparkled back at her.

'It's beautiful,' she murmured huskily. For a second her mind flew back to when she had been wildly in love with Greg. How she had longed for him to ask her to be his wife... How thrilled she would have been to have his ring on her finger.

'So, what do you say, Abbie?' He leaned forward. 'Shall we give it our best shot?'

She met his dark gaze, and there was a moment's silence. Then she shrugged. 'I suppose I don't have any choice, do I?'

'There is always a choice.' He stood up and came round towards her. Her heart beat wildly in her breast as he reached for her hand and pulled her to her feet.

'What are you doing?' Her voice sounded as breathless as she felt.

'Sealing the deal with a kiss, of course,' he replied easily. 'Didn't Rachel complain that we didn't kiss enough.'

Before she could make any reply, he had pulled her forcibly into the hard circle of his arms.

'Don't... don't, Greg.' Nervously she put a hand up against his chest. 'This is silly, this——'

She never got to finish the sentence. Greg's mouth came down on hers with a hard, almost hungry, force.

She tried to push herself away, telling herself she hated this assault on her senses. Telling herself she hated this man.

His lips softened, plundering hers with inviting sensuality.

Immediately a knife-sharp heat spiralled inside her and her lips started to respond of their own volition, her body pressing closer to the almost magnetic power of his.

'It's going to be all right.' He whispered the words against the softness of her skin as he pulled away from her.

Was it? Her heart was thundering, her emotions in total disarray. Somehow she doubted those words.

CHAPTER EIGHT

'THAT'S exactly right,' Margaret assured Abigail, as she walked out of the changing-rooms in the silk suit.

'Are you sure?' Abigail turned to look at her reflection. The suit was a pale pink and made of Thai silk. The jacket was long and the bodice fitted neatly into her small waist, outlining her slender curves. The skirt was straight, with just a small split at the back.

'You don't think I should go for something a little more simple in design?' Abigail asked, as she turned to look at Margaret again. 'I mean, we are only having a small, low-key wedding. I don't want to overdo it.'

Margaret shook her head. 'You look stunning in that suit. Greg will love you in it.'

Abigail sincerely doubted that. No matter what she wore, Greg was not going to love her. That was not what this wedding was about.

Her spirits dampened by that thought, she turned anxiously towards her reflection. She felt very unsure of herself and of the boundaries of her relationship with Greg.

There had been a period a long time ago when she had longed for this. She had dreamt of choosing her wedding-dress, of gazing into Greg's eyes as she made her vows. She had never for one moment dreamt that she would marry him in these circumstances.

Her heart thumped painfully as she remembered the way he had kissed her on the evening she had accepted his proposal. She hated to admit that she had enjoyed the feeling of his mouth against hers, the warmth of his

115

body pressed close. She closed her eyes, willing herself not to be so foolish. The kiss had meant nothing... This wedding meant nothing. It was all for the children.

She mustn't be misled by the fact that Greg was being so utterly charming to her at the moment. It suited him to act out this charade. The awful thing was that sometimes she did start to forget that it was a charade. In fact, sometimes, when she allowed herself to relax around him, she could almost forget how he had hurt her... and remember the man she had thought she had loved.

Greg did have a gentle side that she had almost forgotten about, and he could still make her laugh... Heaven knew that was an achievement in itself these days. And the girls adored him.

It never failed to amaze her how they idolised their uncle. He was a very strong force in their lives. Maybe Jenny had realised that when she had left him joint custody.

Sometimes, when she lay in bed and thought about Jenny and Mike, she wondered what they would say if they could see her now. Would they approve of this union? Would they agree it was wise and in the best interests of the girls?

The shop assistant interrupted her thoughts as she brought out another dress for her to try on.

'No.' Abigail shook her head as she looked at the long, romantic white dress. 'I'll take the suit.'

What did it matter? she thought, as she returned to the fitting-room to take the outfit off. Greg wouldn't notice what she was wearing, anyway. Strangely, that thought tore at her heart.

When she got dressed again in her navy blue trouser-suit and returned outside, she found Margaret buying a beautiful négligé.

'Margaret, I hope that's not for me,' Abbie said quickly, as her eyes took in the sexy silk gown edged with creamy lace.

'Of course it is,' Margaret said firmly. 'Greg gave me strict instructions that I was to get the best for you. Why do you think he opened several accounts in the best stores?' She grinned wickedly as she turned to pick up an Oscar de la Renta suit. 'How about this for going away?'

'No, Margaret.' Abigail cast an uncomfortable look at the very smart saleswoman who was hovering around them. 'Anyway, we are not having a honeymoon, just a few days in New England with the girls.'

'Of course it's a honeymoon,' Margaret cut across her forcefully. 'I just wish you would agree to my having the girls for you. You need some time on your own.'

Abigail shook her head. She had already been through this with Greg. She wasn't prepared to leave the girls, even for a few days. 'It's good of you, Margaret, but you are going to be busy getting ready for your trip to Florida.'

'Yes, but——' Margaret started.

'No buts,' Abigail cut across her forcefully.

'You are one determined lady,' Margaret said with a laugh. 'But I still think this suit would look perfect on you.' She held the outfit up temptingly. 'What do you say?'

Abigail shook her head. She didn't like the fact that Greg had insisted on buying all her clothes for the wedding. But, short of making a scene in the shop, there seemed little she could do at the moment. She did, however, resolve to pay Greg back as soon as she could. 'Really, Margaret, I have enough.'

'Oh, well.' With a disappointed sigh, the older woman put the suit back. The sales assistant also looked disappointed, Abbie noticed wryly. Not that she had any

reason for such a long face; they had spent a fortune in
here in the last hour.

'Would you like us to deliver your purchases to Mr
Prescott's address?' the woman asked now.

Margaret nodded. 'That would be great. As you can
see, we are already laden down with bags.'

At least all this was bringing a smile to Margaret's
face, Abbie thought with a sigh, as they turned to leave
the opulent shop. The happy thought of a wedding
seemed to have lifted the deathly pallor from her skin
and she seemed to be enjoying helping Abbie to get ready
for the big day.

They hadn't told Margaret the real reason they were
marrying. Apart from anything else, she had been so
over the moon about their news that they hadn't wanted
to destroy her pleasure.

Even though the sun was shining, it was bitterly cold
outside. They walked a little further along Fifth Avenue,
looking in shop windows, but Abbie noticed that
Margaret was flagging a little now. 'Shall we go and get
some lunch?' Abbie glanced at her watch. She was supposed to be meeting Greg at his office in about three-
quarters of an hour, and they were going to collect the
licence for their marriage.

Margaret also glanced at her watch. 'No, I think I'll
get back to the apartment now, Abbie,' she said briskly.
'Why don't you go on ahead and meet Greg? Perhaps
the two of you can have lunch together.'

'Well...' Abigail hesitated. Greg hadn't invited her
for lunch and she didn't like to take anything for granted
where he was concerned.

Before she had time to say anything, however,
Margaret was hailing a cab. 'I'll drop you off on the
way,' she said, as a yellow cab immediately pulled in
beside them. 'And don't rush back for the girls. I'll pick
them up from school.'

Abigail grinned at her future mother-in-law. 'I'm supposed to be making life a bit easier for you, Margaret, and instead you are rushing around like crazy helping me.'

Margaret smiled. 'It's my pleasure, Abbie,' she said softly. 'I'm just so happy about you and Greg. I think you will be the perfect wife for him.'

'I hope so,' Abbie said quietly. Inside she had hundreds of doubts about that. 'At least the children are pleased about everything,' she continued in a more positive tone.

'Oh, yes,' Margaret laughed. 'It's done us all a power of good after such a bleak period.'

A few minutes later the yellow cab pulled up outside the impressive Prescott building and Abigail stepped out on to the pavement with more than a few misgivings.

'I am rather early, Margaret,' she said hesitantly. 'Do you think it will be all right?'

Margaret laughed. 'Greg will be thrilled to see you. His eyes light up every time you walk into the room.'

Abigail smiled at that. 'You are just a romantic, Margaret Prescott,' she said, with sparkling eyes.

'Nonsense, I know my own son.'

A smile still played around Abigail's lips as she turned and walked into the building. She didn't kid herself that Greg was in any way infatuated with her. She knew why they were getting married and she didn't try to romanticise the situation, but maybe things would work out. They were getting on well these days, and Greg could turn out to be a warm, considerate partner.

The reception area that Abigail entered was extremely luxurious. Her feet sank into the soft thickness of the red carpet, and she noticed with admiration the skilfully arranged vases of exotic flowers that adorned the long desk.

There were four receptionists behind that desk, and Abigail noticed that each one of them was very attractive and very well groomed. Were good looks a necessary requirement to get a job working for Greg Prescott, she wondered drily? Somewhere at the back of her mind she found herself remembering Connie, Greg's beautiful fiancée from all those years ago. She remembered Connie saying that she was well aware of Greg's wandering eye for the ladies, that she tolerated it.

Abigail pushed the distasteful thought well away as one of the girls asked if she could help her.

'I'm Abigail Weston,' she said briskly. 'Mr Prescott is expecting me.'

The beautiful blonde glanced down at a book in front of her. 'Have you got an appointment?' she asked in a rather sceptical voice. 'Because I'm afraid I can't see your name in his appointment book.'

'Yes.' Abigail replied calmly. 'I'm Miss Weston.'

As that obviously didn't mean anything she added, 'I'm Greg's fiancée.'

That statement certainly created a stir of interest. Every woman behind the desk turned to look at her, weighing her up from the smart navy blue suit to her gleaming blonde curls.

'Mr Prescott's fiancée?' the blonde asked now in a startled tone.

Abigail fought down a feeling of annoyance. 'Perhaps you would ring up and tell him I'm here?' she suggested in a brisk tone.

The girl shook her head. 'I'm very sorry, but Mr Prescott is still out to lunch.'

Abigail frowned. 'Well, perhaps I can wait for him?' she asked, after a moment's uncertain pause.

The woman pursed her lips. 'Well, I couldn't say when he will be back. He has cancelled his other appointments for today.'

Abigail was saved from having to make a reply to that by the sound of Greg's voice as he came in through the doors behind her. She turned with a feeling of relief, a smile lighting her face. It was a smile that faltered and died immediately, as she noticed that Greg was not alone. Jayne Carr was clinging tightly to his arm.

'Hello, Abigail.' Greg seemed not one whit put out by her presence. 'How long have you been here?'

'I've just arrived.' With a strong effort of will, Abigail made her voice bright and airy.

'There, darling, I told you that we were in time,' Jayne said with a smile as she looked up into Greg's eyes. 'We could have had another coffee.'

Abigail couldn't believe the wave of anger that swept through her at that remark. Obviously it wasn't a co-incidence that Greg had arrived back here at the same time as Jayne. They had been out having lunch together. Now she knew why he hadn't offered to have lunch with her.

She tried to stifle the feeling of resentment. After all, why should she care whom Greg preferred to have lunch with? It should mean nothing to her.

Even so, for all her staunch words, it did grate on over-sensitive nerves to know that he preferred to lunch with another woman.

'As it turns out, it's a good job we didn't have another coffee,' Greg said easily, then added, 'You've met Jayne, haven't you, Abbie?'

'Yes, we have met.' Abigail held the frosty note out of her voice with tremendous difficulty. She was aware of the row of receptionists behind her, listening to this conversation with interest. No wonder they had looked startled to hear Abbie was Greg's fiancée. They must all have known he was lunching out with Jayne... They probably knew that he saw a lot of the other woman—more than was strictly necessary for work, anyway.

The woman looked very poised and extremely beautiful in a cinnamon-coloured suit. Her make-up was perfect, her hair, although extremely short, was somehow very feminine, very chic. She smiled at Abbie now. 'Congratulations, by the way. Greg has been telling me all about your plans.'

Just how much of his plans had he been telling her? Abigail wondered. Had he told her why he was getting married? Somehow that idea was very upsetting.

'Has he?' It was all she could think of to say.

'I've just been trying to wangle an invitation out of him to the wedding.' Jayne looked coyly up at Greg. 'But he keeps telling me that it's just a small ceremony— that he doesn't want any fuss.' She rolled her eyes. 'To hear him talk, it's all very low-key. Typical of a man's attitude, I suppose. Leave things to them and they want the minimum of fuss, minimum of romantic touches.'

Abigail's heart felt cold as she listened to the woman. She supposed she shouldn't be surprised that Greg was unenthusiastic about their wedding; she just wished he wouldn't make it so obvious to Jayne. For some reason, it made Abigail feel hurt and rather foolish. She had to swallow hard before speaking. 'Well, it will be low-key, but you are very welcome to come if you want, Jayne,' she said steadily.

'Thank you. I will look forward to it.' The woman smiled at her in a friendly fashion, then stood on tiptoe to kiss Greg's cheek. 'Thanks for lunch, Greg. I'll catch you later.'

Abigail hated herself, but all kind of weird emotions were eating away at her as she followed Greg towards the elevators.

She felt furious that he had so blatantly had lunch with his girlfriend, and a horrible cold suspicion was growing suddenly inside her mind. Did Greg intend to be faithful to her once they were married? Or did he intend to continue in his old womanising ways?

They travelled up to the top floor of the building in silence. Abigail couldn't even bring herself to look at Greg. When the doors opened, he led the way down a long corridor and into a room where a girl was sitting working on a computer.

'This is my private secretary, Elaine Goodison.' Greg introduced her swiftly. 'Elaine, this is my fiancée, Abigail Weston.'

Abigail was subjected to another startled glance from another very attractive young girl with long, thick dark hair.

'Will you bring us through some coffee, Elaine?' Greg continued briskly as he headed for the door to his private office. 'And hold all my calls.'

'I thought we were in a hurry to leave,' Abbie murmured as she made herself comfortable in the leather chair he directed her towards. 'Haven't we an appointment at the city hall or something?'

'Well, as you are early, there are one or two points I want to discuss with you first,' he said crisply, as he took the seat across the desk from her.

She shrugged. 'Fire away.'

'Have you rung Charles?' he asked casually, as he leaned back into his chair.

Her eyes met his across the desk. For a moment she was taken aback by the question. 'Yes . . . I rang him a couple of nights ago.'

'And?'

She frowned. 'And what?' What on earth had Charles to do with anything, she wondered?

'What was the outcome?' he asked patiently.

Her eyes drifted over him for a second. He looked very much the hard attorney. His dark suit seemed to intensify the blackness of his hair and eyes. His mouth was set in a firm line. There was no softness in his expression, no hint of warmth. Looking at him now, she could almost laugh at the naïve thoughts that had been floating around in her mind earlier about him making a warm and considerate partner. She must have taken a short leave of her senses.

Sometimes Greg seemed like a total stranger to her. She never knew what was going on behind those cool, watchful eyes. It was difficult to believe that in a couple of days' time she would be his wife.

She swallowed hard and had difficulty gathering her thoughts together. 'I told him we were getting married,' she said briskly. 'What else could I tell him?'

For a moment her mind locked on the conversation she had had with Charles. She had been very upset; the last thing she wanted to do was hurt Charles. The ironic thing was that she had told him he deserved more than she could give him...that he should only settle for someone who loved him totally. Her mouth twisted in a bitter line now as she held Greg's cool watchful gaze.

'What else indeed?' Greg murmured drily.

'He was upset but very understanding.' Abigail bit down on her lip as guilt flooded through her.

'Very sporting of him.' Greg's voice was derisive.

'Whatever you might think of Charles, he is a decent man.' She jumped quickly to his defence. Charles had been very good about everything. Abbie had given him a key to her apartment before she left, and he had promised to continue to keep an eye on it until she could get back to sort things out.

'So he didn't break down and cry or anything when you told him you couldn't marry him?' Greg continued in a sardonic tone.

'I don't find that question remotely amusing,' she said coldly.

He shrugged. 'I don't give a damn how amused you are. I just want to tie up loose ends.'

'Was that what you were doing over lunch?' she asked drily. As soon as she had voiced the question, she wished she hadn't. The last thing she wanted was to appear jealous. He would find that very entertaining.

'Ah...' He drawled the word lazily and, much to Abigail's fury, a hint of amusement did creep into his tone now. 'Do I detect a hint of jealousy?'

'Don't be absurd. I couldn't care less,' she grated furiously. The awful thing was that, as she spoke the words, she was very well aware that they were a lie. She cared more than she wanted to—more than she could understand. Perhaps it was her pride, she told herself quickly. After all, no one liked to be made to look foolish.

'Do what you want. Just don't try to cross-examine me. I may be marrying you, but I will never belong to you.'

A terrible silence followed that remark. Greg watched her from eyes that glittered dangerously, and she knew that she had overstepped the mark. That she had somehow succeeded in shattering that remarkably cool exterior of his.

'Make no mistake, Abigail, you will belong to me in every sense of the word after Saturday.' He spoke in a low tone that was gravel-hard.

A shiver raced down her spine at those words, but she forced herself to meet his eyes. 'Don't count on it,' she said softly.

'Oh, but I do.' Calmly he slid open a drawer next to him and took out a file. 'And, being an attorney, I leave nothing to chance.'

There was silence in the room as he opened the file and started to leaf through it. Abigail bit down on the softness of her lip. She had a curiously numb feeling inside her as she waited for him to speak again.

'I had one of my colleagues draw up a marriage contract for us,' he said briskly. 'I want you to read it carefully. Take it to an attorney if you feel you need some independent advice.'

Abigail couldn't find her voice to make an answer to that. Although he had spoken of a contract once before, she hadn't really taken him seriously. She realised now that Greg's gentle manner towards her recently had lulled her into a false sense of security. She had started forgetting the lessons she had learnt about him in the past, had started to forget this cold, calculating side of him. She had never thought it possible to hurt so much as she did at that moment.

She was incredibly relieved when there was a tap at the door just then, and his secretary brought in a tray of coffee. It gave her a moment to try and collect her thoughts.

'That's all right, Elaine,' Greg said swiftly, as the girl started to pour their drinks for them. With a nod, the girl turned and left them.

'So.' Greg handed a sheaf of papers across to her. 'Glance at it and ask any questions you want. We can discuss it in detail later.'

She took it from him with unwilling fingers. She didn't want to glance at it and she certainly didn't want to discuss it. She made a pretence of looking through it as he poured their coffee, but she couldn't see a word; her eyes were misted with tears.

'Don't you think this is going a bit far?' she asked at length, when she had taken a few shaky breaths and quelled the feeling of unbearable sadness.

'It's best to be prepared for any eventuality,' he said nonchalantly.

'You weren't in the Boy Scouts by any chance, were you?' she managed to grate sardonically as she flicked over the pages again with unseeing eyes.

He ignored the comment. 'You'll find that a lot of the clauses are to your advantage,' he said briskly.

'Who says?' She glanced up at him as an awful thought struck her. Had Jayne drawn up this contract? Did she know everything? Her stomach twisted at the thought. It seemed very likely that might be the case. Probably that was what they had been discussing over lunch.

'I do.' He spread his hands. 'But as I said, take it to an attorney of your own choosing and get it checked over.'

'How about Jayne?' she couldn't help herself asking. 'Do you think she would advise me?'

For a moment his eyes narrowed. 'I would advise you to take it elsewhere,' he told her coolly. 'Out of my firm completely.'

Her eyebrows lifted sarcastically. 'Not a very good advertisement for the Prescott name,' she drawled, with just a tinge of bitterness in her tone.

'I'm trying to be unbiased,' he told her levelly.

'Of course you are,' she grated sarcastically. 'Greg Prescott always likes to seem unbiased and fair in all things, including marriage and divorce and money,' she rattled on, and at the same time she was willing herself to shut up. She was sounding foolish, she knew it, but she was hurt and she wanted desperately to lash out and hurt him back. 'So what's the bottom line?' She lifted the papers and waved them airily in front of him. 'What key points in this delightful wedding-gift would you like to draw to my attention?'

He shrugged. 'There is no need to take it quite so personally, honey,' he drawled. 'As they say—a verbal agreement isn't worth the paper it's written on. That——' he nodded at the papers '—just clarifies things.'

She held his gaze with mutinous eyes. 'What exactly does it clarify?'

'How much money I will pay you if our marriage fails,' he answered her calmly. 'That if our marriage does hit the rocks, you will not be entitled to take the children——'

'Oh, you've covered every angle, haven't you, Greg?' Her voice shook with the force of angry emotion inside her. It seemed that, no matter what happened, she would never win with this man.

'You've got to see it from my point of view,' he said calmly. 'You could marry me, let some time elapse, then run with the children to England and Charles. I must safeguard against that.'

'Not to mention running away with your money,' she grated sardonically. Did he really think she was that devious? she wondered miserably. 'You've got it all your own way, haven't you, Greg?' she said now.

'I'm the one making the rules, honey.' He held her gaze steadily. 'If you don't like them you can always go back to England.'

Her heart slammed with ferocious strength against her breast as she reached for a pen. 'I'll keep that in mind, thank you,' she said, with a coolness she was proud of. She signed her name with brisk flowing strokes, before looking up and fixing him with a defiant and penetrating stare from clear eyes. 'But just remember this: hurt me or the girls, and I'll make dust of your papers.'

He inclined his head. 'That is not my intention,' he said on a gentler note.

What was his intention? she wondered bitterly. It was obvious that he didn't trust her, that he still regarded her as a shallow, money-loving person. How on earth could they ever keep a marriage together when it was blatantly obvious that neither of them trusted the other one inch? It was like playing Russian roulette.

CHAPTER NINE

SUNSHINE spilled brightly down from a clear blue sky as Abigail stepped out of the white Rolls Royce.

She looked extremely beautiful in the delicate silk suit. Her blonde curls were caught back with orchids and she carried a delicate spray of roses.

It was her wedding-day. It should have been the happiest day of her life, yet her spirits were heavy with doubt.

It was strange, but she kept thinking about the conversation she had had with Charles a few days ago. She had told him he deserved better than she could offer him... that he should only marry for love.

Yet here she was making a very pragmatic decision about her future. Did she know what she was doing? she wondered for the millionth time as her nerves stretched inside her. Taking a deep breath, she tried to chase her doubts away.

The girls and Margaret were waiting for her inside the foyer of the luxurious hotel where the ceremony was to take place.

Both Rachel and Daisy looked very pretty. They wore white organdie dresses with pink satin sashes and pink flowers in their hair. They were smiling happily as Abigail came across to them, as was Margaret.

'You look so beautiful,' Margaret murmured happily. 'It's wonderful, it really is.' For a moment tears sparkled in the older woman's eyes.

Greg appeared in the doorway behind his mother and Abigail's gaze immediately moved to him. He looked sensational in a dark grey suit and silver-blue tie. His hair gleamed raven-black under the subdued lighting of the hotel. Her heart caught painfully as their eyes locked, and then his gaze moved slowly over her appearance.

'You look sensational,' he murmured softly, as his eyes came back to rest on her face.

She felt herself blushing and tried very hard to control the feeling. He was only being polite, she kept telling herself impatiently. People expected the bridegroom to compliment his bride. He was only doing what was expected.

He held out his arm. 'Shall we go through, Abbie? The judge is waiting for us.'

Abigail nodded. She was about as ready as she would ever be.

Judge Silas Barnes married them in a quiet service in the centre of a vast hall that was decorated in an old baronial style.

As Greg slid the ring on her finger and the judge declared them man and wife, Abigail had the feeling that it was all a dream, that at any moment she would wake up back in England.

She turned to look up at her new husband with wide sparkling eyes, and he smiled at her in a way that was somehow reassuring. Then he bent his head and his lips touched hers in a warm sensual caress that was over almost before it began, leaving her feeling even more dazed, her heart thudding even more erratically.

After that everyone crowded around to congratulate them. There were only a few guests, and Abbie noticed that Jayne was among them. The woman looked stunning in a vivid blue suit, a large-brimmed hat perched elegantly on her well-groomed head.

'Good luck, darling,' she murmured huskily as she stood on tiptoe to kiss Greg's cheek.

Abigail looked away sharply and tried to close her mind to the doubts that once more surfaced where Jayne

Carr was concerned. She wondered if the other woman was upset today...if she had secretly harboured dreams of marrying Greg one day? And what about Greg—would he continue to see the other woman secretly?

Abigail bit sharply down on her lip and looked down at the children.

'Is that it now?' Rachel asked with a frown. 'Are you married?'

'Yes, darling.' Abigail had to laugh; it was hard to believe that something so momentous could happen so quickly.

'So now you can stay with us for ever and ever,' Daisy put in happily.

'Something like that,' Abbie agreed with a smile. It was worth everything just to see those two little girls happy, she told herself firmly. She had done the right thing.

'I hope you won't be homesick for England,' Jayne cut in smoothly. 'It will be a strange feeling knowing you can't go home. Altogether different from being on holiday. I'd say you will find it difficult to adjust.'

'I'm sure I'll manage with Greg by my side.' Abbie smiled sweetly at the woman. But deep down she wanted to get the message across that Greg was now her husband, her property.

'I'm sure you will,' Jayne said smoothly. 'Greg is a wonderful guy. I wish you all the best, Abbie.'

Suddenly Abigail felt sorry for this woman. She knew what it felt like to have a broken heart...to dream a dream and then have it smashed.

'Thank you.' Abigail smiled warmly.

A member of staff announced that cocktails were being served for them in the other room. With a feeling of relief, Abigail turned away from the other woman.

'Everything all right, Mrs Prescott?' Greg caught hold of her arm as she passed him, and she looked up at him with a shy smile.

'Everything is fine . . . thank you.'

'So polite,' he murmured, and there was a husky note to his voice now as he reached and touched her face. 'Did I tell you how beautiful you look today?'

'You did mention something earlier.' She tried to keep her voice light, but it was hard when her heart was fluttering like a wild thing inside her.

When Greg looked at her like that she found it hard to think straight.

'Come on, you two love-birds,' Margaret said with a laugh beside them. 'You will be on your own soon enough.'

Those words sent a shiver of apprehension racing down Abigail's spine. The thought of being alone with Greg, of sharing his bed again, was making her feel almost nauseous with nerves.

Somehow Abigail got through the next couple of hours with a smile firmly fixed on her face. There were drinks, and then a delicious meal was served for them.

Toasts were proposed, and Greg was called on to make a speech. He took it all in his stride, laughing and joking and entertaining everyone with his dry wit.

Then, in a more serious vein, Greg looked down at Abigail and his eyes were warm as he met her sparkling blue gaze.

'Jenny once told me that Abigail would make the perfect wife for me,' he said, with a small smile playing around the firmness of his lips. 'I took that as a very high compliment because I know Jenny loved Abbie with all her heart.' Greg looked away from her and down the line of his friends. 'So I think we should drink a toast now to our absent family, Jenny and Michael, because, although they are not here with us in body today, I'm sure they are here in spirit.' He lifted his champagne glass. 'Jenny and Michael.'

It took all Abigail's self-control not to cry. She felt hot tears prick behind her eyes and blinked them furiously away.

She lifted her champagne glass with a trembling hand and then caught Rachel's sweet smile across the table from her.

Everything was going to be all right, she told herself firmly. She was staying with the girls, she was married to Greg, and she was going to make it work.

Abigail's positive mood seemed to falter and die a few hours later, as they flew to their honeymoon destination. She kept remembering Greg's words about making love. He had said he wanted a normal marriage, but how could that be possible? she wondered angrily. How could she make love with a man who didn't love her? It was against all her principles.

You've done it before, a small voice whispered inside her. That was different, she told herself fiercely. Back then she had imagined herself in love with Greg and she had believed he had returned those feelings. Their love-making had been dynamic, passionate in the extreme, but she couldn't possibly feel like that again.

She flicked a glance at Greg as he started to put the helicopter down. What was he thinking? she wondered. Like her, he had been very quiet since they had left the reception at the hotel. His mind seemed preoccupied with something... Perhaps he was thinking about Jayne? It was hard to tell anything from his expression; the hard rugged features were inscrutable.

'Well, here we are, home sweet home,' he said, as the noise of the engine faded into the silence of the night.

Abigail looked up at the house. Lights blazed a warm welcome against the cold night sky, and golden pools of colour spilled over the hard frosty lawns.

'Come on, honey,' Greg murmured gently. 'You look tired.'

She felt exhausted, but she wouldn't for one moment admit that. 'I'm fine,' she said lightly, and started to unfasten her seatbelt. 'Actually, I'm not a bit tired.'

'If you say so.' For a moment his eyes moved gently over her.

She had changed into a warm suit before they left the hotel. It was a rich Titian red, yet despite the vibrant colour and the fact that she wore a matching lipstick, her skin looked chalk-white, her eyes wide pools of turbulent blue.

She felt herself grow hot under his scrutiny and she turned away to look at the girls. They had fallen asleep the moment they had taken off in New York, and they were still flat out.

'I think we should get the girls inside,' she murmured softly. 'They are exhausted.'

'I'll put the travel rug around them and carry them in,' Greg said swiftly, and reached for the door-catch.

They walked up to the house in silence. Abigail came to a surprised halt when the front door opened and a middle-aged woman met them with a beaming smile. 'Welcome home and congratulations.'

'Thanks, May.' Greg grinned at her. 'Meet my wife, Abigail.'

Somehow Abigail managed to return the woman's friendly smile and say something polite.

'May is my right-hand woman,' Greg explained as he carried on into the house and up the stairs with the girls. 'May and her husband Jack keep this place running smoothly for me. I couldn't do without them.'

May laughed. 'Your husband is a charmer, you know,' she said to Abigail as she turned towards the kitchen. 'I'll just get Jack to bring in your luggage.'

Charming was not the word that sprang immediately to mind, Abigail thought crossly. He had deliberately led her to believe that he had no housekeeper last time they came here. What had been the idea? she wondered, as she followed him up the stairs. Had he been testing out her skills in housekeeping? Her blood boiled at the thought.

The girls woke slightly as Greg put them down on their beds, and for a while Abigail turned her thoughts to undressing them ready for bed.

May tapped on the door just as she was tucking them in.

'Jack put all the cases in your room, Mr Prescott,' she whispered softly. 'Is that all right?'

'That's fine, thank you, May.'

For a moment the housekeeper's eyes moved over the sleeping children. 'Poor little things,' she murmured sadly.

'They are coming through it,' Greg said steadily. 'Abbie has really done wonders with them.'

Abbie turned, surprised at such warm words of encouragement.

May nodded. 'Well, I just wanted to say that I would like to help with them. Don't feel you have to get up with them in the morning. I will see to their showers and breakfast.'

'That's very good of you, May,' Greg said warmly.

'I'll enjoy it,' the woman said honestly. 'And besides,' she added with a gleam in her eye, 'it is your honeymoon.'

Abigail tried not to blush at those words.

'Now, is there anything I can get you?' May went on briskly. 'Something to eat? A drink?'

Greg looked across at Abigail.

She shook her head. 'No, thank you, May.'

A little while later, as they closed the door on the girls and crossed the corridor, she found herself wishing she hadn't turned down that offer—anything to put off being alone with Greg.

'I thought you said you had no housekeeper,' she said, as soon as May disappeared towards the stairs.

He laughed. 'I never said that. You just assumed it.'

He opened the door into a beautiful bedroom. A log fire roared in the large fireplace, sending a warm terra-cotta glow over mink-coloured carpets and the silken sheen of damask fabrics on a large brass bed. A crystal vase filled with Michaelmas daisies and yellow-flowered winter jasmine sat on the dressing-table. The room was lightly scented with the flowers and pine from the fire.

But Abigail's attention was held by the sight of that double bed. She stood just inside the door and tried to keep her mind away from it and on the subject in hand.

'So why didn't you correct my assumption? And where was May, anyway?' she demanded in a low-pitched, angry tone.

'I don't know why you are getting so irate,' he said calmly as he opened his suitcase. 'As a matter of fact, May was attending her daughter's wedding.'

'Oh!' For a moment that deflated her anger, leaving her feeling slightly foolish. 'Well, you could have told me.'

'Why?' He turned to look at her. 'You coped beautifully, anyway.'

'What was it—some kind of test of my housewifely skills before you popped the question?' she asked bitterly.

He laughed at that. It was a genuine sound of warm amusement. 'You don't really believe that...do you?'

She glared mutinously at him.

'For heaven's sake, Abbie, your housewife skills have never been an issue. I can afford to hire all the help you need. The only thing I care about is your capacity to love and support your family.'

That statement threw Abigail for a moment and she just stared at him.

'Are you going to stand there all night?' he grated sardonically. 'You look like a door-stop. You can come and sit down, you know. This is your bedroom as well as mine now.'

'I know whose bedroom it is,' she muttered under her breath as she moved forward to open her suitcase. It was his, it would always be his. She didn't feel like Greg's wife; she felt like some stranger who had inadvertently stumbled into someone else's life.

She sat down on the bed and her eyes moved around the room. It was very luxurious and somehow blatantly sensual. She swallowed hard and tried to concentrate on the practical side of things. 'Which is my wardrobe?'

He nodded to the fitted cupboard opposite her and she rose swiftly to hang her clothes away.

When she opened the doors, however, she found the cupboard already half-full of women's clothing.

She fingered a silk blouse, and then her hand ran over a full-length fur coat. 'Who do these belong to?' She turned questioning eyes on her husband, who had finished unpacking the few items he had brought and was walking round the bed towards her.

'You, of course. I thought you would need them as most of your clothes are back in England.'

For a moment she was struck speechless as her eyes moved back over the exquisite selection of clothes. She noticed that the Oscar de la Renta suit that Margaret had selected on their shopping trip was hanging between a Chanel suit and a trouser-suit by Chloe.

'It's very kind of you, Greg,' she stumbled at last. 'But I really don't need you to buy my clothes for me.'

'Anything you don't like you can change. I've opened you several accounts at some good stores,' he said calmly.

'It's not a case of not liking them.' She turned to look at him, her eyes beseeching him to understand. 'It's just that I've always bought my own clothes...always been independent.' She shrugged helplessly. 'This...this makes me feel like a kept woman, somehow.'

He met her eyes steadily. 'You're my wife, Abigail. At the risk of sounding old-fashioned, I want to "keep" you.' He moved closer to her and reached out a hand to touch her face. 'I don't mean that I have objections to you continuing with your career,' he told her gently. 'I will help in any way I can if that's what you want. But I do want to be able to indulge you a little—just call it an old-fashioned whim of mine.'

Her heart was thudding in a most erratic way at the husky tone of his voice and the light seductive touch of his fingers against the smoothness of her face.

'I...I don't know what to say,' she mumbled at last. Her mind was clouded with confused thoughts as she stared into the darkness of his eyes.

'Don't say anything.' A small smile played around the firmness of his lips as he reached behind her and took out an item of clothing. 'But you could always slip into something a little more comfortable.'

Her eyes followed the filmy wisp of a nightdress that he tossed casually down on to the bed, and her cheeks lit with delicate colour.

'It's only a suggestion,' he said, as her gaze met his again and he noticed the vulnerable, almost timid, light in her eyes. 'I want to make you happy, Abbie.'

She swallowed hard as he lifted a finger to touch the trembling softness of her lips. 'Things used to be so good between us,' he said huskily. 'I hope, if we both try to please each other, they can be good again.'

Then he turned without another word and left her alone in the room.

Her legs felt so weak that she had to cross the room and sit down on the edge of the bed. Her heart was thundering as if she had just run a race, her throat felt dry, her lips even dryer. The only sounds in the room were her heartbeat and the soft crackle of the fire.

She didn't understand Greg sometimes... He could sound so gentle, so caring. She couldn't place the strong emotional current that had just surrounded them. It had been sexual, yes... but there was something else.

She reached out a trembling hand and lifted the night-dress that sat next to her on the bed. It was so silky-sheer as to be almost transparent. She dropped it, her heart racing again, her feelings so confused that she couldn't think straight. About anything.

If she tried to meet Greg halfway, could they possibly stand a chance of having a happy marriage?

She didn't trust Greg, she told herself forcefully; she knew from past experience what sort of a man he was. Yet over the last few weeks she did have to admit to a growing respect for the way he treated the children. He had shown himself in a different light... He had shown himself capable of caring and loving.

But he didn't love her, she reminded herself, for all his talk about wanting to make her happy. They had married only because of his love for the children.

Her hands curled into tight fists. This was getting her nowhere. She could sit and try to analyse things forever without success. The facts were that she was now Greg's wife. She had made a bargain and that bargain had in-cluded her sharing his bed. The deed was done. Now all that remained was for them both to make the best of a bad situation. If that meant trying to please each other, trying to be friends, then so be it.

With a look of determination on her face, she lifted the nightdress and headed for the bathroom.

She didn't linger under the warm jet of the shower but stepped briskly out and dried herself, before releasing her hair from the combs that had held it up away from the water.

Then she slipped on the nightdress and regarded her reflection in the brightly lit mirror.

As she had suspected, the garment was completely transparent. The firm uptilt of her breasts was clearly defined, the rosy outlines of her nipples distinct against the white silk.

She bit down on the softness of her lip, and her eyes were huge blue pools of anxiety in the porcelain paleness of her skin.

Perhaps if she hurried into bed before Greg came back into the room, he wouldn't see her in it properly. She had no doubt that once he joined her in bed the nightdress would quickly be discarded anyway.

A shiver of apprehension raced through her as she turned for the door. She wouldn't enjoy their lovemaking. It would be a sham, a mockery of what she had once felt for Greg, but she would endure it, and perhaps, if she was lucky, find a little solace for the unhappiness and the loneliness in her soul within his embrace. Taking a deep breath, she opened the door.

She had hoped to find the room empty, but to her consternation Greg was sitting on the edge of the bed, fully dressed, sipping a glass of champagne.

He glanced up and his dark eyes moved with slow, cool deliberation over her body. With a thrust of anguish she realised that she might as well have been standing naked in front of him. The bright light from the bathroom silhouetted her figure perfectly in the white silk. He could see every curve, every inch of her from the tips of her toes to the healthy sheen on her blonde hair.

She didn't know whether to move forward or to retreat, so she just stood there like some frightened, cornered animal.

'Very beautiful,' he murmured, his voice deep and husky.

The sound seemed to unlock her paralysis and, despising herself for her fear, she dragged her eyes away from him and reached out a hand to switch the bathroom light off. Now all that lit her was the soft glow of the fire and one delicate lamp.

'Champagne?' He held out a long-stemmed crystal glass towards her.

Trying not to notice the way he was looking at her, she moved gracefully into the room. She was more than a little annoyed by the tremble of her hands as she took the glass from him.

'I'm not going to bite you, Abbie.' His voice was gentle. 'Come and sit next to me.' He patted the silk cover beside him.

Feeling like a child, she obediently did as he asked. She sipped her champagne and the frothy bubbles soothed the dryness of her throat.

'What shall we drink to?' Greg held up his glass.

'How about the children?' Abbie asked huskily.

He nodded. 'Daisy and Rachel, then.' The glass gave a soft melodic ring as it brushed against hers.

He took a sip of the liquid and then put the glass down. 'Talking about children...' Calmly he reached into the drawer beside him and lifted out a packet of contraceptives. 'I took the liberty of bringing these. I don't know how you feel, but——'

'That's fine.' She cut across him briskly, embarrassed and deeply, deeply distraught at his cool, almost remote, attitude.

What was going on behind the dark watchful eyes? she wondered with a tingle of nerves bordering almost on hysteria. Obviously he didn't want to risk getting her pregnant for all his talk of a normal marriage. What did he want from her? An occasional roll in the sack when the mood took him, and a gentle mother-figure for the girls? Was that it?

She finished her drink. 'Is there any more champagne?'

He lifted the bottle of Moet from the ice-bucket and refilled her glass. 'Shall we drink to our future this time?' he asked, as he put the bottle down without topping up his own glass.

She tossed back half of the glass before turning to look at him. 'Do you think we have one?' she asked directly as she met his dark gaze.

'I sincerely hope so.' His reply was crisp and succinct. 'I wouldn't have married you otherwise.'

She shrugged. The champagne was making her feel a little light-headed, or was it fear that caused that awful muzzy feeling? Whatever it was, she suddenly felt like screaming at Greg. Anything to ruffle that cold exterior, anything to get some kind of human reaction from him. Surely he was regretting this now? Surely he was thinking about Jayne? About what he had given up?

She bit down on her lip, restraining the urge with such difficulty that she trembled violently.

'Abbie?' He took the champagne glass from her hand, his eyes concerned. 'Are you all right?'

'Of course.' She forced a lightness to her tone that certainly wasn't inside her. Then she met his eyes and took a deep breath. 'Well, shall we get it over with, then?'

One dark eyebrow rose. 'I beg your pardon?'

'It's not like you to be coy, Greg.' She gave a brittle laugh that was edged with more than a little tension. 'I'm talking about the sex bit—it was part of your bargain, remember?'

'Oh, yes, I remember.' His voice was very cool now. He leaned over and put her glass down before turning to look at her again.

His face was dark and impassive. There was no flicker of emotion in the hard glittering depths of his eyes.

Damn him to hell, Abbie thought with furious rancour. Why didn't he lose that tough coldness? Didn't he have any doubts about the rights and wrongs of what they were doing?

Sex for Abbie was making love, she couldn't separate the two things in her mind, therefore it seemed totally wrong to make love with someone without the love element being present... Perhaps that was one of the reasons she had never been able to give herself to Charles.

'So let's get it over with,' she forced out through suddenly dry lips.

'You sound as if you are going to lie back and think of England.' Greg's voice held just an edge of sharpness. 'Or is it Charles you will be thinking of?'

She swallowed hard as he said those words. Part of her would have liked to retaliate and ask if he would be thinking of Jayne, but she couldn't voice that question... she was far too afraid of his reply.

She looked away from the dark intensity of his eyes. 'Does it matter?' she said with a light shrug. Obviously Greg couldn't give a damn, anyway.

Silence descended for a moment except for the soft crackle of the fire. 'I don't suppose it does,' he said at last, a hard note of finality in his tone. 'All right, if that's how you want it to be...' He got up from the bed and took his jacket off. Then he unbuttoned the white silk shirt.

Abigail's eyes followed his movements in a kind of panic-stricken haze.

The fire glowed over the powerful contours of his shoulders and the flat planes of his stomach. His skin, still tanned from the summer, was like burnished copper in the firelight...

He reached for the fastening of his trousers and she turned her eyes away. 'Greg...stop.' Her voice came out in a whispered rush. 'I didn't mean it.'

He stood still for a moment, then turned to look at her. She met his gaze with wide, shimmering blue eyes, then buried her head in her hands, her silky blonde curls falling around her face in a protective curtain. 'I can't go through with this, Greg... I just can't.' To her horror, she started to cry, the tears streaming down the paleness of her cheeks in a steady, warm torrent of emotion. All the pent-up anxieties, all her mixed-up, wild thoughts just seemed to come to a head and explode.

'Don't cry, sweetheart.' His voice was unbearably gentle and that just made her cry harder.

She felt the bed give as he came and sat down next to her. Then his arms were round her and he pulled her into the protective warmth of his embrace soothing her as if she were one of the children, rocking her backwards and forwards and stroking her hair with exquisite tenderness ...

'I'm sorry, Greg.' Her breath caught in painful sobs. 'I don't know what's the matter with me.'

'No, I'm the one who's sorry.' He whispered the words huskily against her ear. 'You're still grieving, and you're very unsure of what we've done...' His hand moved from her hair to the silky material at her back, stroking down her spine in comforting, gentle circles. 'I've been an insensitive pig tonight—especially asking you to wear that nightdress.'

For some reason her womanly pride rose at those words and her head jerked up. 'Do I look silly in it?' she whispered in a trembling tone. Her eyes were so misted with tears that she couldn't see his face. He was just a dark, blurred smudge of colour.

'Of course you don't look silly in it,' he said swiftly. 'You look beautiful in it, more beautiful than I ever remembered you.' His voice lowered to a husky tone. 'I just shouldn't have asked you to put it on. We need to take things slowly, get used to each other again.'

'I suppose so.' She wiped at her tears, feeling incredibly foolish... incredibly vulnerable...

He stood up and she immediately felt bereft and cold without the warmth of his arms, although she knew the room was warm.

He returned in a moment with a box of tissues and handed her one.

'Thank you.' She dabbed gently at her eyes. 'I'm really sorry, Greg... I'm behaving like a fool.'

'No, you're not.' He reached out a soothing hand and stroked a stray curl from her forehead. 'You are behaving like a woman.'

Her lips twisted in an attempt at humour. 'Isn't that the same thing in a man's eyes?'

'Not in this man's eyes,' he said softly.

For a moment their gaze locked and Abigail felt her breath catch painfully in her throat again. Her eyes lowered to his chest. The dark hairs glistened with the dampness of her tears. Impulsively she reached out a hand and stroked them away.

His skin felt taut under the softness of her fingers. She liked the feel of him. Memories rose vividly, memories that she had locked away in the deepest recess of her brain. Memories of their bodies joined together in powerful harmony. She swallowed hard and abruptly withdrew her hand.

'Would you like me to sleep in the other room?' he asked in a low tone.

Her eyes flew towards his face and, as they locked with the beautiful darkness of his eyes, she knew with complete certainty that that was one thing she did not want.

Wordlessly she shook her head.

His mouth twisted in a half mocking, half bitter smile. 'You want to get the dreaded deed over with, I take it?'

Silence fell as Abigail desperately tried to clear her mind. It wasn't that at all. She wanted Greg ... The need was so deep that it shocked her to the core. She wanted to feel his arms round her. She wanted him to hold her and kiss her and make passionate love to her.

'I didn't say that.' She whispered the words softly, and she knew that the blue of her eyes held an invitation she dared not voice.

Greg met her eyes. Then gently he reached across and touched her face.

Impulsively she lifted a hand to cover his, holding it and then turning her head to kiss it softly.

'Abigail?' He whispered her name, and then his lips found hers in a soft feather-light caress that sent shivers of desire racing through her.

She moved closer, longing for his kiss to deepen, longing to feel his body against hers.

'Almost like old times,' he murmured against her ear. 'It used to be so good....'

'Yes...' She moaned the word softly. She remembered exactly how good... She remembered the powerful sensations with a sharp, thrusting longing that made her almost dizzy. She nuzzled her head in against his neck, breathing in the clean, familiar scent of him.

Then his head moved and his lips found hers in a hard, hungry, demanding kiss that sent her emotions reeling in delightful chaos. Suddenly she forgot everything but the powerfully sensuous sensation of being in his arms.

His hands moved down over her body, pushing the flimsy material of her nightdress to one side, and his fingers stroked over the satin smoothness of her breasts, making her moan with ecstasy.

'Let's get rid of this, shall we?' He murmured the words huskily, and with expert ease he lifted the night-dress and pulled it over her head.

Her hair caught in the silky material for a second and then fell in soft tumbling waves around her creamy bare shoulders.

He pulled back from her for a moment, his eyes raking over the slender curves of her naked figure with a gleam of male appreciation.

'You are very beautiful, Abigail Prescott,' he whispered softly, dispelling the brief moment of shyness she had begun to feel.

He reached out a gentle hand to cup delicately the fullness of her breast. Then he lowered his head, taking one rosy, hard nipple into the warmth of his mouth.

The feelings inside Abigail were so fierce, so exquisite, that she gasped his name out loud and stretched her arms up, running her hands over the smoothness of his back, then up into the thick darkness of his hair.

When his lips left her body her eyes flew open in protest. She felt wild with longing as she watched him move back from her.

Firelight played over the rippling muscles of his shoulders and arms as he pulled the damask cover back from the bed and then lifted her gently between cool, scented sheets.

Not a word was spoken as he removed his trousers and joined her in the infinite comfort of the deep double bed.

Abigail's heart was beating so loudly that she felt sure he could hear it.

His hands moved over the soft, curving shape of her figure, then his body moved over hers and she could feel the hard, naked pressure of his skin against hers.

She closed her eyes, overwhelmed by the exquisite sweetness that flowed through her body. I love you, Greg Prescott, she thought with bitter-sweet clarity as his body entered hers.

CHAPTER TEN

WHEN Abigail woke up, she was lying tightly entwined in Greg's arms, her head resting on his broad chest.

The room was in darkness except for the flickering orange flames from the fire. They played over Greg's face as he slept, highlighting the strong, handsome features, the sensuous curve of his lips.

Warm, wonderful sensations spiralled deep inside Abigail as she remembered the way Greg had made love to her earlier.

How could she have forgotten how passionate Greg was? How could she have forgotten such deep fulfilment?

She pressed her face against his chest and kissed his warm flesh. How could she have forgotten how much she loved him? The realisation that she still loved Greg was so new, so wonderful, that she hugged it to herself like a secret talisman.

Did Greg love her? The question hovered for a moment in her mind before she squeezed it out. She knew the answer to that—she had always known that Greg did not love her. Perhaps that was why she had denied her love for him so completely, so vehemently, over the years that she had come to believe the lie.

Tonight she had come face to face with the truth and, although it shocked her, right now it also made her feel a whole lot happier about her marriage. She did love her husband, and surely that fact would help her to try and make this marriage work, not just for the children's sake but for her and Greg as well. Maybe if she tried really, really hard, Greg would grow to love her.

She cuddled even closer against him, the only sound the soft rise and fall of his breathing and the occasional crackle of the fire. She closed her eyes and, for the first time in weeks, fell into a deep, tranquil sleep.

When Abigail woke up again, daylight was streaming into the bedroom and she was alone. She stretched languidly in the large double bed, wondering where Greg was and feeling a little disappointed that they hadn't woken together.

She remembered again the warm passion of the night before. It seemed like a distant dream now... too good to be true.

'Good morning, sleepy-head.' Greg's voice coming from the doorway made her heart jump.

'Good morning.' Feeling a little self-conscious, she pushed her blonde hair out of her eyes and, holding on tight to the silk sheets, turned over to look at him.

He was fully dressed in dark brown cords and a brown and cream heavy jumper. 'I brought you a cup of tea. If I remember rightly, you always did like tea first thing in the morning.'

'Yes...' Did he really remember that or was it a lucky guess? Holding on tight to the sheets, she tried to sit up while keeping her nakedness covered.

It was ridiculous to feel shy—after all, Greg had explored every inch of her body last night—but she did feel awkward.

'Thank you.' She took the china cup and saucer from him and then found she couldn't lift the cup to her lips without letting go of the sheets. She felt her cheeks grow hot with embarrassment as she met his eyes.

He grinned. 'Having difficulties?'

She shook her head. 'No. No, of course not.'

He grinned all the more, and then sat down on the edge of the bed. 'If you lean forward I'll adjust your pillows,' he offered crisply.

She did as he asked, her eyes lowered from his gaze as he came very close. The familiar aroma of his cologne made her heart miss a beat and, to her consternation, her body trembled with desire as his hands inadvertently brushed her shoulders.

'There... Is that better?' He leaned away from her again, his manner brisk.

She nodded. 'Thank you.'

'You've gone back to being very polite all of a sudden.' His eyes raked over his skin, noticing the flushed, rosy heat in her cheeks, the vivid sparkle of her eyes. 'I didn't hurt you last night, did I, Abbie?'

'No...' She shook her head and averted her eyes from his, uncomfortable with the subject. It was one thing to admit to herself how she felt about Greg, but she didn't want him to find out—at least, not yet.

She wanted to take things slowly, try to evaluate how he felt about her. After all, she had her pride and she didn't want Greg to know she was a complete push-over where he was concerned. He might find her amusing or, worse, he might take advantage of her vulnerable heart.

'Where are the children?' she asked, glancing at the bedside clock and seeing to her horror that it was nearly ten.

'May has taken them into town with her,' he said easily.

'Into town?' She sat bolt upright now, all thought of modesty forgotten.

'Don't panic. It's a sleepy village just down the road, and May and the girls are getting on like a house on fire. I trust the woman implicitly.'

Abigail leaned back, mollified by that. She knew that, if Greg trusted the woman, she would be all right.

The shrill ring of the phone interrupted the private moment, and with a sigh Greg reached to pick the receiver up from the bedside table.

'Greg Prescott.' He spoke briskly, his manner vaguely impatient. 'Oh, hi there, Jayne.' His tone softened as the caller identified herself. 'No . . . it's all right, you are not interrupting.'

Abigail felt a shiver of cold reality wash over her at those words. Yes, she was interrupting, she wanted to scream. How dared that woman ring on the first morning of their honeymoon? This was supposed to be a private time.

With a sigh she slipped out of the bed while his back was turned, and went into the bathroom to run herself a shower.

She didn't care about Jayne Carr, she told herself firmly as she stood under the forceful jet of hot water. She wasn't jealous . . . She had no need to be. Greg was married to her now.

Feeling a little better, she reached for a towel and wrapped it firmly around her body before going back into the bedroom.

Greg was still on the phone. He turned slightly as she came into the room, and his eyes followed her movements as she opened the wardrobe to select some clothes.

He covered the mouthpiece for a moment. 'Wear some riding-gear, honey. We'll take a ride as it's a nice day.'

Abigail didn't get a chance to make a reply because he launched straight back into his conversation with Jayne.

'No, don't worry about it,' he said easily. 'Look over the police reports again and ring me later.' He laughed warmly at her reply. The sound made Abigail's blood-pressure rise dramatically.

She found a pair of fawn jodhpurs and a cashmere cream polo-neck, and turned angrily for the bathroom again.

Her heart was thudding erratically as she started to get dressed, and she hated herself for the emotions racing through her. She was jealous of Jayne Carr—jealous that Greg had so much in common with her, that he could talk so easily to her.

She reached for her hairbrush and pulled it through her long blonde hair with hard, almost ferocious, strokes. Then she glared at her reflection in the mirror and tried to think rationally.

Jealousy was not an emotion she was familiar with and she hated herself for it. Greg was just discussing work, that was all, she told herself firmly. She was being totally ridiculous getting so upset about it.

To be fair to herself, she was still adjusting to the realisation that she still loved Greg. Her mind had been clouded with so much emotion lately that it was hard to think straight about anything.

'Abbie?' Greg tapped on the door. 'Can I come in?'

'Yes.' Taking a deep breath, she forced the negative jealousy out of her mind and turned to smile at him as the door opened.

'Sorry about that,' he said, coming to stand next to her at the vanity-unit. 'Jayne is taking over one of my cases for me, and it's rather complex.'

'That's OK.' She was pleased at how light her voice sounded, as if she really didn't care.

His eyes swept over her slender figure in the tight-fitting jumper and trousers, and he gave a low whistle. 'You look very delectable in that outfit, Mrs Prescott.'

She smiled shyly. 'Thank you.'

He reached across to kiss her lips with infinite gentleness, then grinned. 'Come on, let's get some breakfast and get a ride in before the children come back.'

'Shouldn't we wait for the girls?' Abbie asked anxiously.

'The girls will be having a whale of a time.' Greg turned to lead the way downstairs. 'I guarantee that May will be spoiling them rotten.'

They were just finishing a delicious breakfast of maple syrup waffles and hot fresh coffee when the phone rang again.

'Get that, will you, honey?' Greg said absently, as he turned from loading the dishwasher.

As the receiver was just next to her, Abigail picked it up quickly and read the number out.

'May, is that you?'

Abigail stiffened as she recognised the dulcet tones of Jayne. Did the woman have no sensitivity? she thought crossly. She wouldn't dream of disturbing people on their honeymoon with so many calls.

Abigail identified herself briskly.

'Oh, hi there, Abbie. Are you enjoying your break?'

'Very much, thank you.' Despite the interruptions, Abigail thought wryly.

'That's good. I had a fabulous time there last fall. It sure is beautiful.'

Greg had brought Jayne here! Abigail didn't know why that should hurt so much; after all it was a whole year ago. But, incredibly, she was filled with pain. The thought of Greg sharing that bed with Jayne blinded her with complete jealousy.

'Anyway, I'm sorry about this.' Jayne's tone was anything but apologetic. 'You'll be thinking that, even on his honeymoon, Greg spends more time with me than you...'

Abigail bristled even more at those audacious words. 'I wasn't thinking anything of the sort,' she said lightly.

'Good job.' Jayne laughed. 'I suppose it's something you will have to get used to. I'm afraid I can't do without your husband's expertise.'

It was all said in a joking way, but Abigail wasn't in the slightest bit amused. 'Hold on. I'll get him for you,' she said drily. Then held out the phone towards Greg. 'Jayne,' she told him abruptly.

'Thanks, sweetheart.' Greg closed the door of the dishwasher and turned the programme on before turning casually to take the receiver from her.

'I'll leave you to it.' Annoyed beyond words, Abigail grabbed her coat from the chair and headed out of the back door.

The autumn sun was low in the sky and there was an atmosphere of chilled, misty sweetness in the air. Abigail breathed deeply, trying to rid her mind of the anger and the suspicions that Jayne Carr seemed to be able to generate so easily.

She was being foolish, she told herself again and again. Greg's affair with Jayne was in the past now. They were discussing work, and there was nothing more to it. He was married to Abbie now.

But he didn't love her, she reminded herself fiercely. There was nothing to stop him from carrying on his relationship with Jayne.

The trees had lost their vivid sunset-coloured leaves, which crackled underfoot as she walked across the lawn towards the stables. Desperately she willed herself to think rationally. Surely Greg wouldn't stoop so low as to continue with that woman once he was married? She would have to forget Jayne and concentrate on how much she loved Greg. Concentrate on ways to deepen their relationship.

May's husband was saddling two horses ready for their ride. He turned as she walked across the courtyard towards him, and he introduced himself with a smile.

Jack Roberts was a pleasant man, and he obviously loved horses. He chatted amiably about the mare he had selected for her to ride, and Abigail felt herself starting to relax again as she patted the horse. She was being highly imaginative about Jayne, she told herself, and tried to wipe the episode from her mind.

When Greg came across to join them she had succeeded in burying her treacherous fears, and she managed a smile as he apologised for the delay.

'How long is it since you've ridden?' Greg asked, as he mounted his black stallion and led the way slowly out of the cobbled yard.

'Years . . .' Her voice trailed off as she remembered that the last time was when she had been dating Greg. It had been a beautiful English summer day and Greg had taken her out to the countryside.

Abigail remembered the day vividly: the scent of honeysuckle and roses, the sleepy drone of bees, the way they had laughed together.

They had cantered across a lush green meadow and then tethered the horses to a tree while they sat on the banks of a river. Greg had leaned across and nibbled her ear. 'You're so beautiful,' he had whispered huskily. 'And I love you with all my heart.'

For one crazy moment her eyes filled with tears. It was no wonder that she had deliberately closed her mind to past memories of her time with Greg. Even now, six years down the line, they still upset her.

'Charles doesn't like riding, I take it?' he continued idly.

'Not much, no.' It took all her will-power to keep the tremble of emotion out of her tone, but even so he glanced round at her, his eyes narrowed on the bright shimmer of her eyes.

'Come on, I'll race you down towards the lake,' she said briskly, and urged her horse forward.

Fortunately the mare possessed a good temperament and she responded instantly to Abbie's commands. Once out in front of Greg, she was able to pull herself together and brush the sparkle of tears from her lashes.

Her blonde curls streamed behind her as she urged the horse to go even faster, and the cool air whistled past her ears so that all she could hear was the thunder of hooves on the frosty ground and the thud of her heartbeat...

Of course Greg caught her up with ease, and they both reached the lake at about the same time.

'You're still a skilled horsewoman, I see,' he remarked as they turned their horses to walk more sedately along the banks of the lake.

'I suppose it's something you don't forget.' She patted the mare's neck absently.

'What about Charles?' he asked abruptly. 'Is he something you can't forget either?'

'Charles?' She turned wide blue eyes on him, surprised at that question.

'I couldn't help noticing that you looked upset when I mentioned him a moment ago,' he said nonchalantly.

She frowned, annoyed with herself for showing her emotional thoughts so clearly to him. She wondered what he would say if she told him the truth, that her distress had been caused by memories of him, not Charles? He would probably find that amusing. It would certainly feed that male ego of his no end.

Much as she loved Greg, she would never expose her vulnerability to him... She couldn't risk his mocking smile, his dry comments. It would make her feel so foolish... it would break her heart.

'It's your imagination,' she answered briskly. 'I wasn't even thinking about Charles.' She nodded towards a lane that curved away through the forest on their right. 'What's up there?' The question was asked in a desperate attempt to change the subject.

'A sugar-house. They are used during sugaring season in the spring.'

To her surprise he let the subject of Charles drop. It wasn't at all like Greg. He was nothing if not perceptive, and she knew he was capable of going straight for the jugular, in true lawyer mode.

For a while there was silence between them, but it was comfortable silence. The lane wound through deep tree-lined gorges. The air was fresh with the scent of pine and the only sounds were the steady clip-clop of the horses' hooves and the occasional silvery gurgle of a clear mountain brook.

'We're on the edge of the White Mountain national forest here.' Greg spoke suddenly. 'If you look up you can see the slender white birch trunks from which the mountains are named. In the summer their green leaves ripple with those of the brown sugar-maple. It's an unforgettable sight.'

'You really love it out here, don't you?' She dragged her eyes away from the beauty of the countryside to look over at him.

He smiled. 'After the rat-race of the city, it's a tonic.'

'Have you ever considered moving out here full-time?'

'It would certainly be a better place in which to bring the girls up.' He shrugged. 'But there are a few things to take into consideration... Maybe one day.' He turned his horse. 'I suppose we should head back. The girls will be home soon and wondering where we are.'

Abigail turned to follow him silently. Was Jayne one of those considerations, she wondered bleakly? Living in New Hampshire would certainly make an affair more difficult.

With difficulty she pushed Jayne Carr firmly from her thoughts.

CHAPTER ELEVEN

CHRISTMAS shopping in New York was fabulous. Abigail couldn't believe the shops and the decorations—it was all just magical.

It was less than a week before Christmas, and bitterly cold. The sky was a heavy, misty grey and the light started to fade by early afternoon as if a storm was brewing. But the shops were bright orbs of colour against the grey of the weather. Everything from tinsel and baubles to giant Father Christmas displays glowed in the windows.

Abigail completely forgot the time in F.A.O. Schwarz, on Fifth Avenue. It was a magical toy-store, with clowns and toy soldiers and performers costumed as Raggedy Ann roaming around the premises. Every toy imaginable was in there, and she got completely carried away buying all sorts of wonderful things for the girls.

As a result, when she looked at her watch she got quite a shock. She only had an hour to buy herself a dress for this evening's party and get home and changed.

The thought of the firm's Christmas party did not fill her with delight. It wasn't that she didn't like parties— it was just this particular party, and all because Jayne would be there.

She sighed, and tried to dismiss the thought as she lifted a hand to hail a cab. So what if Jayne was there, she asked herself sternly? It was nothing to her.

Except that over these last few weeks, she had been trying to forget that woman's very existence, a little voice reminded her.

Two cabs sailed past her in quick succession and she sighed despondently. Her parcels were heavy and, despite her warm coat, she was freezing cold. Perhaps she shouldn't bother with a new dress. She had her black velvet one and there was a midnight-blue one that Greg had bought for her as part of her trousseau. It was only lack of self-confidence and the knowledge that Jayne would probably look stunning that were driving her to buy something new.

A cab stopped beside her and she heaved a sigh of relief.

'Where to, lady?'

There was no time to dither, with the meter ticking and an impatient cab-driver waiting to get back into the stream of traffic. Impulsively she gave the address of a boutique on Madison Avenue that Margaret had recommended. She would just have a quick look, she decided briskly.

The traffic was always bad, but tonight it seemed particularly grim. To make matters worse, it started to snow, lightly at first and then more and more heavily. White flakes flurried through the dark sky, covering the cars and pavements in cotton-wool white.

Thank heavens Margaret had gone to Florida, Abigail thought absently as they sat in a traffic jam and the weather grew worse and worse. And thank heavens Greg was taking some extra time off work for Christmas. She settled back against the car seat with a smile. They had promised to take the children to New Hampshire for the festive season, and they were to leave the day after tomorrow. The thought of having so much time with her husband was enough to shut out the chill of the day.

As the cab turned into Madison Avenue and slowed down outside the Gianni Versace boutique, Abigail glanced at the blizzard outside and had second thoughts about getting out.

She was just about to tell the driver to forget it and take her home, when she noticed that the car parked just up the road from them was a silver-blue Mercedes like Greg's. She frowned as she noticed the personalised number plate. It was Greg's car! What on earth was he doing here?

The thought had no sooner crossed her mind than the door of the boutique opened and two people hurried out into the snow. One was her husband, the other was un-mistakably Jayne Carr.

Abigail's breath caught painfully in her chest, and she barely registered the irate cab-driver telling her he hadn't got all day. Her eyes and her senses were firmly tuned on the couple dashing towards the Mercedes.

Jayne was wearing a full-length fur coat; snowflakes sparkled against the dark fur and the darkness of her hair. She laughed as she slid slightly in the snow and Greg's arm immediately went round her, steadying her and holding her tightly against his side until they reached his car and he opened the passenger door for her.

Abigail felt almost nauseous with anger and jealousy as she watched him help Jayne carefully into her seat before handing her the long silver box he had been carrying from the boutique.

'Lady, have your emotional crisis somewhere else, for God's sakes.' The cab-driver held out his hand. 'I've got a living to make.'

'Sorry.' Abigail's voice didn't sound as if it belonged to her as she turned shimmering eyes back on him. 'I've changed my mind... I... Take me home.' She gave him the address and sat back, her heart hammering wildly, her body so cold it felt frozen through to the marrow.

Over these last few weeks she had foolishly allowed herself to think that her marriage was a success. She had felt so close to Greg. He seemed so loving, so tender. At night when he held her tightly in his arms, she had blotted out all her doubts and allowed herself to dream that he really did feel deeply for her, even though no word of love was spoken.

Her lips twisted bitterly. Would she never learn? Would she never understand that Greg was a master at charming a woman into a false sense of security, at making passionate love without any emotional commitment?

On the surface theirs was a happy, normal marriage. But the reality was that he had married her because he had no other choice.

What had he been doing? she wondered bleakly. Buying Jayne her Christmas present, or a little something to make up for the fact that he couldn't spend Christmas with her this year?

Abigail's mind went around and around the question. She paid the cab-driver and went into the apartment block with a feeling of absolute desolation.

The housekeeper, Alison, was just finishing the ironing. She looked up as Abigail came into the kitchen, and her eyes narrowed. 'You look frozen!' she exclaimed, her eyes moving over Abbie's pallor with concern.

'It's not too good out there.' Abigail found her voice from somewhere and put her parcels on the kitchen table. 'Where are the girls?'

'In the den.' Alison put down the iron and filled the kettle. 'I'll make you some coffee and put those things away for you. You go and sit down.'

Abigail nodded, too tired to argue. 'You'll have to put the parcels at the back of my wardrobe. They are Christmas presents for the girls.'

The children were watching a Walt Disney film, their faces alive with excitement as they lived through the story of Sleeping Beauty.

'Come on, my two beauties, let me sit beside you,' Abigail said lightly as she sat between them on the settee and cuddled their little bodies close. They were deliciously warm against the bleak coldness inside her.

What was Greg doing now? she wondered grimly. Kissing Jayne goodnight? Apologising for not being able to take her to this party tonight? Making love to her?

She cuddled the children even closer. What did she expect? she asked herself furiously. Theirs was a marriage based on necessity. Love had never been part of the bargain. She was just going to have to learn to live with that.

She was in the shower when Greg arrived home. She heard his voice calling to her from the bedroom and she steeled herself to go out and face him as if nothing had happened, as if her heart were not breaking.

She dried herself and wrapped a towel turban-style round her head before putting her robe on and going out to greet him.

'Hello, sweetheart. Sorry I'm late.'

He reached to kiss her, but she turned her head so that his lips brushed the side of her cheek. She just couldn't bear his lips to touch hers, not with the knowledge that Jayne was still warm on them.

If he was surprised by the move, he made no comment. 'So, how was your day?' she asked nonchalantly, not quite meeting his eyes.

'Hell.' His gaze raked over her. 'How about you?'

'I finished the Christmas shopping. I got the girls some fabulous things.' With an effort, she spoke normally.

'Great.' His eyes moved over her face, noting the tired, almost listless, light in her blue eyes and the translucent quality of her skin. 'I'm sorry I couldn't get the time to go with you,' he said softly. 'It's just that things are very hectic at work and——'

'And you have to put in extra time if you want to finish tomorrow,' she finished flatly for him. 'It doesn't matter.' She turned away from him to sit at the dressing-table and dry her hair. But it did matter...especially now that she knew he could make time to go shopping with Jayne. The knowledge stung.

He hesitated for a moment. 'Actually...' he began hesitantly.

Her eyes flew to meet his in the mirror, apprehension clear in their beautiful depths as she waited for him to continue.

But he just shrugged. 'Doesn't matter,' he sighed, and moved away from her to open the bathroom door. 'I suppose I had better grab a shower. We don't want to be late for this party.'

What had he been going to say? Actually I've been with Jayne? Actually, I'm having an affair? Her mind locked into the way Greg had held Jayne so tightly against his side as they laughed their way through the snow. Somehow they had looked so right together. Had Greg come to the conclusion that his marriage was a mistake? Fear spiralled inside her. She couldn't bear to lose Greg out of her life again. The thought was unendurable.

The party was in full swing as they walked through the elegant doors of the downtown hotel.

The place was packed to capacity. People were milling from the large, almost palatial, ballroom where a small band was playing, across the wide reception-hall to where a buffet was lavishly laid out on a long banqueting-table. The ambience was a dynamic mix of big-city power and sophisticated glamour.

Abigail tried to bury the feelings of fear and hurt inside her and smile politely as Greg introduced to her top circuit judges, attorneys, senators, bankers. After a while one name started to merge into another until she had little hope of remembering any of them.

As they moved through the crowds, Abigail caught
sight of Jayne. She looked stunning in a sequinned
cherry-red dress that was worn off the shoulder and ac-
centuated her slender, almost boyish, figure to per-
fection. Their eyes met across the crowd and the woman
smiled. Abigail returned the smile and hoped fervently
that she wouldn't come across to join them.

It was a forlorn hope. A few moments later Jayne was
at their side smiling brightly up at Greg. 'Hello, stranger.'
She stretched up to kiss his cheek.

Abigail felt the knife inside her twist at the easy intimacy of the woman's behaviour. It was only a few hours
since they had seen each other, she thought furiously.
Couldn't the woman put on some kind of front for de-
cency's sake?

'I'd like to introduce Liam Hume to you.' Jayne turned
and, much to Abigail's surprise, drew a tall, good-
looking man forward.

As the introductions were made, Abigail watched the
proceedings with bewilderment and just a dart of hope.
She watched Greg's face as he shook the other man's
hand. Had he known that Jayne was going to bring
someone else tonight? What was Jayne playing at? Was
it a deliberate attempt to make Greg jealous and get him
away from his marriage? That thought brought a cold,
clammy feeling around her heart. It was the obvious
conclusion.

Conversation flowed very easily between Greg and
Jayne for a while. It was hard to tell what effect the
other man had on Greg's emotions. His dark face was
impassive, and he was impeccably polite. If he was
jealous, he was covering it well.

'I take it you are not a lawyer?' Liam looked down
at her as Jayne monopolised Greg with a discussion on
their day in court. He had most unusual silver-grey eyes,

she noticed absently, and a smile that was genuinely friendly.

She shook her head. 'I'm a commercial artist.'

'Really?' He turned towards her more fully, those eyes moving over her slender figure. She was wearing a midnight-blue dress that was dramatically attractive against the porcelain paleness of her skin, and it brought out the deep shade of her eyes.

'I'm in graphic design myself.'

For a while they talked about different aspects of their work. Liam was interesting, informative and engagingly candid, but she found it difficult to concentrate fully on him because she kept trying to hear what Greg and Jayne were talking about—a virtual impossibility over the noise in the room.

'So how long have you been seeing Jayne?' she asked him curiously, when there was a slight lull in the conversation.

He shrugged. 'Not long. I've been asking her out for ages but she always said no. She's been hung up on some other guy for a while.'

'Well, she's going out with you now.' Abbie forced a bright note into her voice. 'Obviously she has fallen for your persistent charms.'

He laughed at that. 'Maybe . . . but I don't kid myself.'

Abigail swallowed hard. Neither did she. The more she noticed the way Jayne looked at Greg, the more she realised that Liam and she were surplus to requirements around here.

Greg and Jayne belonged in the same world. The likes of Liam and herself would always just be outsiders, she realised sharply. And in that moment Abbie just wanted to break down and weep. She loved Greg so much . . . but obviously her love would never be enough.

Greg lifted his head as if sensing someone watching him, and then he was looking directly into her eyes.

For a moment she was reminded vividly of when she had first met him at that party in London. How they had looked into each other's eyes and she had felt the spark of instant attraction. It had meant nothing . . . nothing. She had been a fling then, and she meant little more to him now. Despite that knowledge, despite knowing he was in love with another woman, she still wanted to melt into his arms. Her eyes closed and she looked away, bitterness and contempt for her own weakness welling up inside her.

'So how's married life?' Jayne asked airily, as she noticed Greg's attention had wandered.

'Wonderful.' The note in Greg's voice was warm. How could he be such a consummate actor? she asked herself grimly.

'Have you told Abigail the bad news yet?' Jayne went on briskly.

'Bad news?' Abbie's eyes winged back to Greg, her heart thudding so viciously in her chest that she felt faint.

Greg's eyes were dark and unyielding as they met hers. 'Not yet,' he grated, and there was a roughness to his tone now that deeply disturbed her.

'What bad news?' She could barely contain her anxiety. It was clear in her eyes, in the vulnerable tilt of her head.

'Look—excuse us, will you?' Greg caught hold of her arm. 'I'll just take my wife for a dance.'

Abigail allowed him to lead her through the crowds of people towards the dance-floor. Was it so awful that he couldn't tell her in front of other people? Was he going to be straight with her and tell her he wanted out of their marriage? That seeing Jayne with someone else had finally made him realise the folly of their situation? All these thoughts whirled around in Abbie's head as he turned to take her into his arms amid the swaying couples dancing to a romantic melody.

He touched the softness of her hair and she shivered. 'I'm sorry, honey.'

The softly spoken words were exactly what she had been dreading. Her head jerked upwards and she held his gaze with over-bright eyes.

'I meant to tell you earlier, but you looked so tired when I came home.'

Her breath caught painfully in her throat. This was it. Childishly she wanted to cover her ears. She didn't want to hear... She didn't want him to admit his adultery. She wanted to pretend it wasn't happening, carry on as before. Anything just to have him in her life.

'I'm not going to be able to make New Hampshire until Christmas Eve.'

For a moment she almost laughed with a kind of hysterical relief. The room seemed to spin around in a jumble of wild, blurred colours. She felt dizzy, light-headed with relief and suddenly very ill.

'Abbie, are you all right?' His voice seemed to be coming from a long way away.

She nodded and buried her head against his chest, trying desperately to pull herself together.

'I'm really sorry, sweetheart, I've tried my best but I've got so many people depending on me—I can't let them down.'

Was he talking about clients or Jayne? The treacherous doubts continued mercilessly.

'That's OK, I understand.' She mumbled the words against his chest. The scent of his cologne was so disturbingly sensual that she felt her stomach muscles contract with sudden longing. God, she wanted him now, even knowing that he wanted Jayne.

'Do you?' He tipped her head back and stared down at her. 'I'll make it up to you and the girls,' he said gently. 'I'll take time off after Christmas instead.'

'Fine.' Her voice sounded strange, as if it belonged to some cool, composed stranger.

'I know the girls will be disappointed but...' He hesitated. 'If you want, I'll take you down to the house and you can spend the time there anyway.'

A cold hand seemed to be twisting her heart as if squeezing it of its life's energy. 'What about you?' she asked dully.

'I'll join you on Christmas Eve. It will mean a few days apart, but we can make up for it afterwards.'

So that was it, she thought bleakly. Jayne had won. That was obviously what this was about. Jayne wanted to spend some time with her husband, so they had planned this little ruse together to get her out of their hair for a few days.

'Fine.' She shrugged slender shoulders. 'Whatever you want, Greg.' The words were cool and calmly composed, but, inside, her heart was screaming out, Anything, Greg... I'll do anything... Just don't leave me.

CHAPTER TWELVE

'MRS PRESCOTT, can I make you something to eat?'
May's voice distracted her attention away from the
window, making her realise that she had been staring
out at the snow with empty, unseeing eyes.

She shook her head. 'No...no, thank you, May. I'm
fine.'

The woman's eyes ran anxiously over her. 'You hardly
ate anything at lunchtime,' she said, with a worried
frown.

'Really, I'm fine.' Abigail summoned a brave smile,
even though she knew she looked anything but fine. It
was four days since Greg had dropped them off in New
Hampshire. Four days of wretched unhappiness...of
tormenting ideas about what Greg was doing.

'Can we go for a walk in the snow, Aunty Abbie?'
Daisy looked up from where she was playing with Rachel
by the Christmas tree.

'Please?' Rachel tagged on, seeing her aunt waver
towards saying no. 'We can build a snowman and throw
sticks for Duke.'

Abbie smiled. It took such simple pleasures to keep
the girls happy. 'OK, but you've got to wrap up, it's
really cold out there.'

A little while later, dressed in their thickest, warmest
clothes, they left the warmth of the house for the wild
white beauty of the New England countryside.

It looked like a picture postcard outside: snow covered
the garden and the forests for as far as the eye could
see. The sky was a cold, clear blue and it was reflected

in the ice on the lake, making it look blue-white. The only colours were the bright yellow coats the girls wore, and the red glow of berries, reminding them of nature's warmth.

Together they built a snowman, laughing as Duke kept jumping up against it to try and knock it over. Abigail felt a little better for the fresh air and the children's high spirits. As they walked down towards the lake, she tried to give herself a strict talking-to. There was nothing she could do about Greg... She had to get on with her life, and looking after the girls as best as she could. It was Christmas Eve and Greg would be home in her arms tonight. She had to forget everything else.

'Aunty Abbie?' Rachel cut into her thoughts and she turned grateful eyes down towards the child. 'Will Santa Claus know where we are living this year?' she asked anxiously. 'I mean, will he know that we are not living with Mummy and Daddy any more? Will he know where to bring our presents?'

'Yes, darling.' Abigail smiled reassuringly at the girls. 'Santa knows exactly where you are. He knows everything.'

'That's good.' Rachel hugged her toy rabbit tightly against her and skipped ahead to throw sticks for Duke, who was lolloping along the banks of the lake.

For a while there was just laughter as they threw snowballs for the dog instead of sticks, and he jumped for them, astounded when they dissolved in his mouth.

Abigail looked down at her wedding-ring, wishing with all her heart that Greg was with them. The sound of a high-pitched scream rending the air made her heart stop beating for a moment. For one terrible moment, she thought something had happened to one of the children.

As she lifted her eyes she was tremendously relieved to see both girls standing unharmed just in front of her.

Rachel was crying loudly, but Abigail couldn't see anything wrong.

'What is it, honey?' She bent down beside the little girl, her eyes searching over her to make sure she hadn't fallen or hurt herself. 'What is it?' she repeated, as the child seemed to go almost hysterical.

The little girl was so beside herself that she couldn't speak. Her finger pointed out towards the frozen surface of the lake, and Abigail was horrified to see the child's favourite toy lying a few metres away, well out of reach.

'How on earth did you manage that?' she asked, almost to herself.

'She threw it instead of the stick,' Daisy told her importantly. 'It was a mistake. Can't we just walk on there and get it?'

Abigail shook her head. 'Certainly not. It's dangerous. The ice looks thick, but it could easily break under too much weight.' She looked down as Rachel cried louder than ever. 'Don't cry, Rachel, we will try to get her back for you.' Easier said than done, Abigail thought grimly, as she looked around for a stick to try and reach it with.

After several vain attempts to slide the toy towards her using a long piece of wood, Abigail had to give up. 'Maybe Jack will be able to get it,' she said, looking down at Rachel's forlorn expression with a feeling of doom. Jack had gone into town and it was odds on he wouldn't be back in daylight hours. Already the sun was starting to sink in a cold ball of winter yellow, licking the trees and the snow with faded colour.

'Failing that, it will have to be Uncle Greg.' She lifted the child up in her arms and cuddled her close. 'Don't worry, Rachel sweetheart. We will get Mitzy for you.'

Getting Rachel to bed that night was murder. The little girl cried copiously until her eyes started to look red raw.

At last, with a lot of gentle encouragement and the promise of Santa's visit, she settled into an uneasy sleep.

'I don't think she will sleep the night out,' Abbie said worriedly as she joined May in the kitchen. 'She's absolutely distraught.'

'Poor little thing.' May glanced at the kitchen clock. 'Jack should be here any time now—he's usually back before seven-thirty.' She bustled around making them a hot drink, and put some mince pies on a plate for Abigail.

It was warm and comfortable in the kitchen. The radio was on low and it played soothing music. Abigail relaxed back in her chair. Everything would be all right, she told herself firmly. Greg would be back soon.

Her eyes drifted to the clock, watching it move with agonising slowness. Even though Greg had rung every night, mostly to speak to the girls, she missed him terribly. Her bed was lonely, her thoughts tormented by thoughts of him and Jayne wrapped in each other's arms.

The distant drone of an engine made her eyes fly open. 'Is that the helicopter?' She turned anxious eyes on May for confirmation.

'Sounds like it.' May smiled. 'I'll keep the coffee-pot on, shall I?'

Abigail was too excited to answer. She sprang out of her chair and into the hall, pulling back the heavy curtains and looking up into the night sky with breathless anticipation. After a few heart-stopping moments of doubt, she saw the light of the helicopter as it started to come down.

Greg was home! Abigail's heart sang with happiness. She was just in the process of dropping the curtain when a movement by the lake caught her eye. At first she was going to dismiss it as nothing, but something made her look again.

It was a clear moonlit night. Silver light sparkled on the snow and on the luminous beauty of the icy skeleton trees along the silvery frozen water.

But it wasn't the beauty of the scene that caught Abbie's attention; it was a small, lonely figure standing on the bank of the lake.

'Rachel!' Abigail's heart seemed to somersault over in cold panic. 'Rachel!' She must have screamed the name, because May came dashing out of the kitchen in distress.

'Dear God, Rachel is down by the lake.' Abigail barely managed to get the words out as she wrenched the front door open and raced across the snow down to the water.

The night air was freezing but Abigail hardly noticed it. Her heart was thudding wildly. Her breathing seemed to be coming in desperate gasps. 'Rachel, no!' She screamed the words over and over as she almost fell in her haste to get to the little girl. 'Don't go on that ice.'

She came to an abrupt halt on the bank of the lake. It was too late. Rachel stood a few metres out. All she wore were pyjamas and fluffy slippers. She looked like some Walt Disney apparition in the moonlight, just standing on the ice holding her toy rabbit.

'It's all right, Aunty Abbie, look.' She held up the toy. 'I've got him, I've got Mitzy.'

'Rachel, come back.' Abigail's voice trembled with fear as she held her hands out towards the child. 'Come back nice and slow.'

'You won't be cross?' The little girl hesitated.

'Not if you come back now.'

'Dear God!' May reached her side at that moment, her face draining of colour as she took in the scene.

Abigail wasn't aware of anything except Rachel's progress across the ice. With each little step she took,

Abigail could feel her heart thundering as if all the devils in hell were using it as a baseball.

The child was nearly there when the ice started to move under her feet. 'Aunty Abbie!' she cried out in terror, as it started to break up.

Abbie acted instinctively and without thinking. She darted on to the ice and plucked the child up, throwing her bodily towards May on the bank.

For a moment she thought she had got away with it, but when she lifted her foot to throw herself forward, the ice broke completely and she lost her balance.

Ice-cold blackness was all she remembered after that. Freezing temperatures such as she had never experienced before... So cold it took her breath away, it took all her conscious thoughts away...until all that was left was blackness.

'You little fool, you damned little fool.' The words seemed to be coming from a long way away. They were husky with emotion yet abrasively angry. At the same time rough hands were rubbing her body with fierce, strong, massaging strokes.

For a moment she felt numb and tired—too tired even to open her eyes. The coldness that seemed to have struck through to her bones was abating, though.

'Rachel?' Her eyes flew open as fragmented memory started to return. 'Rachel...where is she? Is she all right?' She struggled for a moment against the warm arms that held her.

'Yes...yes, she's all right. Nothing wrong with her... It's you.' The strong hands were rubbing her again with brisk, firm strokes...strokes that were bringing heat back to her limbs.

She relaxed a little. She was inside the house by the fire in the lounge, she noticed absently, and her clothes were gone. Instead she was wrapped in thick blankets.

She looked up and met dark eyes, eyes that glimmered with some kind of fierce, angry emotion.

'Greg?' She whispered his name with trembling uncertainty. 'Greg...I'm sorry. I didn't know what to do... I don't know how she got down there... I——'

'Ssh.' He cut across her incoherent rambling firmly. 'Ssh.' Then he gathered her against him and just held her tightly as if he was never going to let her go.

Her heart thudded wildly at the closeness. She breathed in deeply, loving the scent of him, loving the feel of his body next to hers.

'Did you pull me out?' She asked the question unsteadily.

'Yes... Another few minutes and it might have been too late.' His embrace tightened instinctively. 'Thank God you didn't submerge completely... But if I hadn't arrived when I did...' For a moment his voice broke with raw emotion.

'Is Rachel all right? Did she get wet?'

'She's as dry as a bone. It was nothing short of a miracle the way you plucked her up. It was incredibly brave...' His voice faltered. 'Hell, Abbie, when I think how I once tried to persuade myself that you only thought about yourself. That you were——'

'Don't, Greg.' She cut across him. She knew what he was going to say—that he had thought her selfish and spoilt. Bitterness twisted her lips. 'At least Rachel is all right.' She closed her eyes as she remembered the full horror of seeing the child standing on that ice. 'She could have died, Greg.' Her voice trembled and tears of emotion filled her eyes.

'And so could you.' He shivered, and then held her away from him to look down at her face. 'Have you any idea how I felt when I saw you stepping on to that ice? Have you any conception of the fear and shock that flowed through me as I ran down towards you?' He shook her slightly as he spoke, making it almost impossible for her to answer.

'God, Abbie... all I could think of was that I couldn't lose you, not again, not like that.'

Abigail stared up at him, her mouth dry, her eyes wide. She felt bewildered by the depth of emotion in his voice, in his eyes. Gently, almost wonderingly, she reached up and touched the side of his face.

'Oh, Abbie.' He seemed to break at that gentle caress and his eyes sparkled with emotion. 'All I could think about was how much I loved you... how much I regretted my stupid pride in not telling you that from the beginning.'

For a moment Abigail thought she was hallucinating. Greg couldn't possibly have said those words... She was dreaming, wishing for them with such fervency that she was mistaking what he was saying.

She stared up at him wordlessly, breathlessly, too afraid that if she spoke she would wake up into reality.

'I know that you are in love with Charles...' He stroked her face, his eyes caressing her with such tender feeling that hot tears started to overflow on to the coolness of her pale skin.

'Oh, darling, don't cry.' He rocked her backwards and forwards. 'I'm sorry, sweetheart. I shouldn't have forced you into marrying me—it was selfish, it was unforgivable. But I just couldn't bear to let you go again.'

The tears fell faster as relief and happiness merged inside her in one incredible emotional explosion. 'Greg.' She breathed his name with trembling feeling. 'I love you so much... You don't know how I've longed to hear you say those words.'

For a second there was a breathless hush, as Greg stared down at her with those deep, dark eyes as if searching her soul, as if he didn't dare to believe what she was saying. Then his lips met hers in a hard, hungry, passionate kiss that stole her breath and her heart.

For a while there was no sound in the room but the crackle of the fire and the pounding of two hearts joined in complete, wild, harmonious passion.

Greg's lips softened and moved to her neck, then her ears, then gently he kissed her tears away.

When at last he pulled away from her, he stared at her with warm, brooding eyes. 'Say it again,' he urged softly. 'Tell me you love me again because I hardly dare believe it.'

She smiled and wrapped her arms round his neck. 'I love you, my darling.' She whispered the words into his ear. 'I'd just like to get rid of these blankets and show you how much I love you.'

'What about Charles?' He held her away from him, his eyes hard again, his mouth set in a grim line. 'You told me you loved him.'

She shook her head. 'I was hurt... I couldn't take the fact that you had cheated on me, lied to me——'

'I beg your pardon?' His voice was abrasively rough as he shook her slightly. 'I've never lied to you in my life.'

She shook her head. 'I knew, Greg... I knew about Connie,' she whispered.

'Knew what, for heaven's sake?' He rasped the words harshly. 'I've already told you that there was nothing between me and that woman—I can't under-stand how——'

'I saw her, Greg,' she cut across him with a shaking voice. 'I saw her at your hotel and she told me everything. How you loved her...how you were engaged to be married.'

Greg shook his head forcefully. 'Listen to me, Abbie. I never was engaged to Connie. Sure, I took her out a few times before I came to England and met you, but there was nothing serious between us.'

'But she told me——'

'She bloody lied.' Greg cut across her vehemently. 'In actual fact, I made it more than clear to Connie before I left the States that we were through. I was frankly astonished when she turned up outside my hotel bedroom door that night, crying and demanding that I came home to her. Quite frankly, I think she was a bit deranged. She had got my address from a mutual friend and flown all the way from the States without any encouragement whatsoever.' He glared down at Abbie. 'My mistake was feeling sorry for her. I let her take my bedroom at the hotel and moved in with Mike because the place was fully booked—she promised to be out of my hair first thing the next morning.'

Abigail stared up at him, hardly daring to believe it was true.

'For God's sake, Abbie. Why would I lie to you now?'

'It's just...she sounded so believable.' Abbie trailed off, feeling totally bewildered. She had believed what that woman had told her for so long that she had real difficulty in adjusting her thoughts.

'I had no idea you had spoken to her,' Greg grated angrily. 'Why the hell didn't you say something? Why didn't you ask me?'

Abigail gazed up at him through a haze of tears. 'Because I didn't trust what you would tell me,' she whispered miserably. 'I didn't trust you, Greg. I'm sorry.'

For a moment her voice broke as she realised what time they had wasted through her stupidity... through her bitterness and pride.

'So you led me to believe you were having an affair with Charles?' He grated the words harshly. 'Were you?' He shook her slightly. 'Were you having an affair with Charles?'

She shook her head, 'No... I was just hurting and I wanted to hurt you——'

'You certainly succeeded in that,' he put in unevenly. 'Even thinking about Charles makes me want to hit someone.'

'I know what you mean.' Her eyes sparkled with tears. 'Jayne Carr has the same effect on me.'

'Jayne?' He frowned. 'She's a business associate and a friend, nothing more.'

'You brought her here to this house...' Abbie trailed off. She didn't want to talk about that woman, she didn't even want to think about her. She wanted to bury her head in the sand and just remember the words Greg had said a few moments ago.

Greg tipped her head so that she was forced to look up at him. 'I lent her my house for a short holiday. I wasn't here at the time.' His dark eyes held hers. 'Ask May if you don't believe me.'

'Oh, Greg.' She pulled away from him and buried her head against his chest. 'I've felt so torn, so unhappy these last few days. My imagination has been working overtime. I thought you were with Jayne... I thought...'

'I was working, Abbie.' He held her tightly. 'And I've hated being apart from you just as much, believe me.' His voice was grim. 'That's why I've decided to give up my work in New York.'

She jerked her head to look upwards at him, her eyes wide.

'I thought I'd take up practice here in New Hampshire—I've already sent out a few feelers.' He stroked her hair. 'I hope that's all right with you?'

'All right?' Abigail reached up and touched her lips to his, happiness bursting inside her. It was more than she could have wished for. Jayne would be a thing of the past...it would be a new start. 'It's incredibly wonderful.'

A knock on the door interrupted them, and May put her head round it. 'Should I ring the doctor for Mrs Prescott?' she asked anxiously.

Greg looked down at Abigail. 'How do you feel?' he asked gently.

'Better than I have in a long, long time,' she murmured with a smile. 'All I need is an early night.'

Greg grinned and looked over at May. 'No, she's fine, thanks, May.'

'Good. Little Rachel is asleep, so you don't need to worry about her.' The woman closed the door and headed off in the direction of her quarters with a knowing smile.

'So... Shall we have that early night?' Greg asked softly as he rose and lifted her into his arms.

'Yes, please.' She cuddled close to him, her heart pounding with anticipation as he carried her easily out of the room and up the stairs.

He pulled back the silk sheets and put her down with infinite care, before unwrapping the blankets from around her body.

For a moment his gaze raked over the slender contours of her body, then he bent his head to kiss her lips, his mouth hungry with passion.

'Hell, Abbie...I don't think this seduction is going to be prolonged,' he growled huskily, as he teased and stroked her quivering body with strong sensuous fingers. 'I want you so much. I've been dreaming of this every night for the last... I was going to say four nights, but really it's been six years.' He grinned down at her and then pulled the covers close around her while he took off his clothes.

'Tell me again,' he demanded, as his naked body pressed close to hers. 'Tell me you love me.'

She murmured the words huskily, her body on fire with desire, her lips clinging to the sweetness of his, her hands stroking the hard length of his powerful body.

'I love you, Greg... I love you.' The words ringing in her ears, she felt the strong thrust of his body as it entered hers.

It was later—much later—when she remembered what day it was. She snuggled closer against Greg's chest and kissed his shoulder. 'Greg... Greg, it's Christmas Eve,' she whispered. 'We haven't brought the presents downstairs for the girls.'

He stirred and kissed her lips. 'Don't worry about it, sweetheart. You go back to sleep.'

She was only too pleased to comply. Her body felt sated, her eyes heavy as lack of sleep from previous nights started to catch up with her. With a contented sigh she rolled over.

It seemed like only a few moments later when the excited chatter of the girls woke her.

'Can I go downstairs, Aunty Abbie?'

She opened one eye to see Rachel standing anxiously beside the bed.

'Now you ask.' Greg sat up and looked at the little girl sternly. 'Shouldn't you have said those words before you went ice-skating last night?'

The child nodded, her bottom lip quivering.

Abbie held out her arms. 'Never do it again,' she whispered against the child's soft cheek. 'Always ask before going anywhere.'

'Can we open our presents now?' Daisy asked impatiently from the door.

Greg grinned and threw Abbie her dressing-gown. 'I don't see why not.'

Together they went downstairs into the lounge. The lights shone brightly on the Christmas tree, glistening over the packages spread invitingly beneath its branches.

With a whoop of pleasure the girls dived to open them.

Greg and Abbie sat on the floor next to them, watching their joy with undisguised delight.

Then Greg turned to pick up a long silver package from behind the tree. 'This is for you, Abbie,' he said softly.

Abigail looked down at the box and her heart leapt as she saw the name of the Gianni Versace boutique.

'I hope you like it,' he said apprehensively. 'Usually I would have enlisted my mother's help when buying you clothes, but with Mother in Florida it had to be Jayne.'

One lone tear trickled down the smooth paleness of Abigail's cheek.

'Abbie? Honey, what is it?' He reached across in concern, wrapping her in strong arms, holding her close.

'Nothing.' She squeezed her eyes tightly closed as waves of relief washed through her. 'It's . . . it's just that I saw you and Jayne outside that boutique . . . I thought you were buying something for her——'

Greg held her away from him, a look of grim determination on his attractive features. 'Abbie, I asked for her help choosing something for you, nothing more.'

'Yes, I realise that now——'

'I hope you do.' He cut across her abruptly. 'Honey, please believe me when I tell you that Jayne means nothing to me. I can't bear to think there are any barriers between us, any mistrust.'

'I do believe you.' Abbie swept a trembling hand across her cheek and met his eyes with a clear, steady gaze.

'Jayne is a nice enough girl, I guess, but she's a fellow-attorney, and I never think of her in any other way.' He shrugged broad shoulders. 'Sure, I've taken her out for dinner occasionally over the years. We talk about work, work and more work.' His dark eyes looked into hers steadily. 'I don't feel one spark of attraction when I look at her. You are the only woman in the world for me, Abbie.' He murmured the words huskily. 'From the first moment I saw you, I wanted you, and you've haunted my dreams ever since. I've never wanted anyone the way I want you——'

He broke off, raking an agitated hand through his hair. 'Of course, I should have said all of this when I asked you to marry me. Instead, my wretched pride and the fear of rejection drove me into trying to force you to stay with me...' He trailed off, his lips twisting bitterly. 'For instance, that awful contract I made you sign.' He shook his head ruefully. 'No wonder you are having difficulty trusting me.'

She swallowed hard, the memory of that ruthless contract still raw inside her.

'I never meant that contract... I never want to hurt you, Abbie. Please forgive me, my darling.' He murmured the words with such sincerity, such deep yearning, that she felt her heart would break with the waves of pure happiness welling up inside her. 'All I want is to make you happy.'

She folded into his arms as any doubts she had had about Greg melted away. She did trust him, she realised without a doubt. 'I've been so blind... There is nothing to forgive,' she whispered fervently. 'I love you, Greg. I love you with all my heart.'

For a while they just held each other, savouring the intensity of the moment.

When Greg pulled back, he reached into the pocket of his dressing-gown and brought out a small jeweller's box. 'Before you open anything else, I want you to open this.' His eyes were deep and steady as they held hers.

With trembling hands she took the box from him and opened it. Inside, a beautiful square-cut diamond sparkled under the fairy-lights with clear brilliance.

'Oh, Greg, it's beautiful,' she gasped. Then she noticed the name on the box was that of a London jeweller. With trembling hands she took the ring out. It was inscribed with her name, Greg's, and a date... It was a date from six years ago!

'I wanted to give it to you the night of Jenny and Mike's wedding,' he said with a self-conscious shrug. 'Unfortunately pride and anger got in the way.'

Wordlessly she stared at him, as he took it from her and slid it on the third finger of her left hand. 'It's a little late,' he murmured. 'About six years too late, but you know what they say—better late than never.'

'Oh, Greg, I don't know what to say.' She breathed deeply, fighting back the tears of happiness.

'Don't say anything, just wear it...always.' He turned and kissed her lips.

For a moment they clung together and it took a while for Abbie to gather her emotional feelings together in order to look at him with clear eyes.

'My present to you seems almost boring now,' she said shyly, as she reached to pick up the gold package from beside her.

To her surprise, he put the gift to one side with hardly a glance. 'I think,' he said seriously, 'that I can wait for my present.'

'Oh.' She smiled shyly at that. 'How long do you want to wait?'

'Well.' He leaned across and whispered against her ear. 'How about nine months, give or take a month? I'm in no hurry, especially now that we've got forever.'